Gun Law of Phoenix Cline

Phoenix Cline had seen the error of his ways and wanted to do something worthwhile with his life. Helping a few indentured Chinese didn't seem like a bad start. But making dangerous enemies by opposing them, or leaving dead bodies behind, is not the smartest way to escape life as a gunfighter. Seeking a peaceful existence and a woman to love are all Phoenix wants. But when men start shooting at him from ambush or come to town gunning for him, the only law he can make them respect is the Gun Law of Phoenix Cline!

By the same author

Gun Law of Phoenix Cline

Terrell L. Bowers

A Black Horse Western

ROBERT HALE · LONDON

ISBN 978-0-7090-9320-6

Robert Hale Limited
Clerkenwell House
Clerkenwell Green
London EC1R 0HT

www.halebooks.com

*For some beloved riders of the range who have gone to the
Great Beyond ahead of me:
My father, James L Bowers rode a truck and
pulled mobile homes.
My brothers-in-law, Calvin Carrico rode a tractor as a
farmer, and Kyle Kleve loved to
ride his Harley Davidson bike.*

Typeset by
Derek Doyle & Associates, Shaw Heath
Printed and bound in Great Britain by
CPI Antony Rowe, Chippenham and Eastbourne

CHAPTER ONE

Silver Springs had been a small, peaceful settlement until the railroad came through. It not only brought drifters and pilgrims seeking work or a new life, it also brought in big business and people seeking their fortunes. The trading post and one-room tavern were quickly crushed out of existence by new competition. Many proprietors sold out for what they could get and left. Silver Springs changed from a quiet, sleepy little burg, into a raucous and rowdy wide open town. A freight and transport company opened up along with a new livery and blacksmith shop. Main street grew rapidly, as a dozen new stores sprang up. Huge casinos offered all manner of entertainment: gambling, music, dancehall girls and cheap whiskey. A large hotel and fancy restaurant, the Palace Inn, opened, as did a lumberyard. A new pharmacy-mercantile was built, to compete with the general store that had managed to survive. Thurmond Hildebrand was one of the enterprising businessmen who owned much of the business district, and he wanted even more.

For a small husband-and-wife business like the Pomeroy House, which sat down a side street and offered rooms and an intimate, small café, the massive growth was a death-blow. They suffered when intense competition and a measure of intimidation closed down the bath house next door. Then the dentist, who lived and worked on the other side of their establishment, was foreclosed on and lost everything he owned. As for Rachel and Grant, they were strapped to survive: pressure and bills mounted, while their business dropped off to almost nothing.

Grant Pomeroy was not ambitious, nor the best of husbands. He had married Rachel at the behest of his father, Nathan, who became ill and forced his irresponsible son to take a wife and settle down. Rachel had wanted to escape the constant hunger and poverty of her own family, plus the drudgery of working sixteen hour days to tend and care for the nine younger children in the family. She had no schooling and few suitors, because she never went anywhere without several children in tow. Nathan Pomeroy offered Rachel's parents fifty dollars, plus a wagon and team, as an inducement for their daughter's hand and they practically dragged her to the altar.

To complete his plan for his son's future, Nathan

put up the bulk of his money to buy the two-storey inn in Silver Springs. He also provided them with a hundred dollars for expenses. It should have been enough to keep them going until the place could earn a living. It would have, if not for the sudden population explosion and competition moving in all along the main street of town. They were left scrambling to pay the bills and Grant soon borrowed to stay afloat. Now he had run out of credit, there was a bank note against the place, and they barely kept food on hand to serve the customers. Worst of all, Hildebrand wanted their property so he could expand his own holdings. He appointed his own man as a judge, then added a sheriff and a couple of bullies as deputies. Considering his wealth and influence, it seemed only a matter of time before Rachel and Grant were pushed out of their home and business.

Rachel worked hard and never complained. It would have done little good if she had, as Grant was taciturn, moody and had never shown any real affection for her. Just the opposite, he blamed her as much as his father for being trapped in a position he didn't like. He had been a happy, shiftless bachelor, wandering about without a care, seldom doing any real work and never forced to shoulder any responsibility. Being burdened with a wife and a business propelled him into a brooding seclusion. With the debts mounting and the added pressure of an ailing father, he began to want nothing more than an escape from his predicament . . . and Rachel as well.

Everything came to a head the day that Blocker Quade and Nape Cod entered their small eatery. The men were Sheriff Martell's deputies, two bullies with badges. Neither had ever taken a meal there before. Even as they sat down at one of the three tables, Rachel experienced a dark foreboding.

Hiding the dread, she took a deep breath and walked over to take their order. At her approach, she suspected they had not come for the daily special. In fact, the two appeared outwardly belligerent and primed for trouble.

'Hi!' she offered, flashing a professional smile. 'Would you two like something to eat?'

Blocker Quade regarded her with a disgusting leer. 'I see something I'd like to taste. How about some tulips.'

Rachel frowned, perplexed, while Nape guffawed loudly and said, 'Would that be flowers you're talking about, Blocker? Or are you wondering how this lady's *two-lips* would taste?'

'I'm not on the menu,' Rachel said timidly, trying to make a jest of their crude behavior. 'We have chuck wagon stew, or we can cook up something for you.'

Without warning, Blocker's hand shot out and he grabbed a handful of her skirt. With a hard yank, he pulled Rachel down on to his lap. She cried out in surprise and immediately swung at his face with a tightly balled fist.

The man was the size of a two-year-old bull and about as strong. Her one blow bounced off of his forehead like she had hit a block of granite. Then he quickly caught up both of her wrists and held them in one meaty paw. Using his free hand, he caught hold of her hair and forced her around, attempting to kiss her.

'Save some for me!' Nape shouted gleefully.

Rachel was completely overpowered, but turned her head away to avoid Blocker's puckered up puss. She tried to kick, but could do little damage when trapped crosswise on his lap.

'Hold still, you little vixen!' Blocker growled. 'This is something I bet you're gonna like.'

'Hey!' Grant bellowed, racing into the room. 'Get your filthy hands off of my wife!'

Grant's reaction to the attack on his wife had been the plan from the start. Blocker rose up to his feet quickly, dumping Rachel right on the floor. As Grant slid to a stop, the big bruiser lifted his massive fists and sneered.

'She's the one who came sashaying over and asked to be manhandled, Pomeroy. If you can't keep your woman happy, don't be yelling at a man who can.'

'Grant!' Rachel cried out. 'Don't! This is what they want!'

But the disgusting insinuation inflamed Grant's

rage and removed caution from his senses. He was only two inches shorter than Blocker, but it was the weight difference and fighting experience that gave the bully a major advantage. At a meager hundred and twenty pounds, Grant was completely over-matched by a man twice his size.

Grant got in one good punch to Blocker's jaw, then the offensive part of the fight was over for him. The big brute hammered away with fists of iron. He knocked Grant back against the nearest wall and pummeled him to a semi-conscious heap. When he slumped to the floor, Blocker hit him several more times. He would have continued the beating, except Rachel grabbed up a chair and broke it over his head and shoulders.

Blocker grunted from surprise and spun about on Rachel. 'Damn, woman!' he snapped, rubbing the back of his neck. 'You could hurt somebody hitting them thataway.'

'Get out!' she screamed. 'Get out of here and leave us alone!'

Nape took Blocker by the arm. 'Let's go, buddy,' he said, flicking a smug glance at Grant broken body, 'I don't think the cook is going to be serving any more meals today.'

Laughing together, they headed for the exit. Rachel dropped down on her knees at her husband's side. He lay in a twisted heap, eyes glassy and unsee-ing. His every breath was labored, exiting his mouth in a raspy wheeze. She placed her hands to either side of his face and realized his jaw was crooked, as if it had become unhinged from one side. Fear and regret tore at her insides. Grant was badly hurt.

Don Baylor, the mayor of Silver Springs, suddenly burst into the room. He grimaced, displaying an immediate agony at seeing Grant on the floor.

'I was afraid.. . . .' He swore softly under his breath. 'I saw those two head this way and I knew. . . .'

'Get Mr Vaughn,' Rachel pleaded. Vaughn had been a medic during the war between the Union and the Confederacy. He wasn't much of a physician, but he was all the town had. 'Hurry!'

'I'm durn sorry, Mrs Pomeroy. I'll fetch him right away.' Saying that, Baylor ran out the front door and hurried up the street.

Rachel felt the weight of the world upon her shoulders. Grant's color was ashen and he was bleeding from a cut above one eye and both his nose and mouth. He came half awake and awkwardly coughed up some blood. Much of it dribbled down his chin as he couldn't close his mouth properly.

Vaughn arrived with Baylor within minutes and the two men carried Grant to the bedroom. The medico worked quickly, while the mayor and Rachel watched and tried to be of some help. After Vaughn had finished cleaning up the blood and doing what he could, he escorted them out of the room. Once out of the patient's earshot, he stopped.

'How'd this happen?' he asked Rachel.

She explained about the two deputies coming in to start trouble. Vaughn listened and he and Baylor were both sympathetic. When Vaughn spoke, there was little hope in his voice.

'It appears Blocker Quade either severely cracked or broke a couple of Grant's ribs. Wheezing like he is, I've got to think one or more of his ribs is busted and the bone has punctured a lung.' He took a deep breath, as if regretting what he had to say next. 'As for his jaw, it's severely broken. I can try to bind it in place, but Grant won't be able to eat anything solid for a long time.' He met Rachel's worry with a grim expression. 'I saw a similar condition once, after a cowboy was kicked in the face by a horse. He died. If you can't eat, you can't survive for very long. Even mashing up food and feeding him through a tube, it's a tough road. I suspect even a surgeon would have a hard time fixing Grant's injured jaw. When compounded by a punctured lung. . . .'

He didn't have to finish. Rachel knew the end result. She remained steadfast, knowing she had only herself to rely on. She would send off a wire to Nathan telling him about his son. However, Nathan's health had gone from bad to worse since she and Grant had wed. The injuries he suffered in the war had taken most of his left leg and he suffered bouts of fever. In his last letter, he said he had a bad cough and the doctor had warned pneumonia might set it. She sincerely doubted he could make the journey from Denver, even by train. It was simply too hard on his frail and ailing body.

Vaughn said he would run over and pick up some pain medication at the pharmacy. Making Grant comfortable was about all they could do for him. The mayor also gave his sympathies again and promised to send his oldest daughter over to help with some of the chores.

Despondent, Rachel went in and sat at the side of Grant's bed. He was half-conscious and each breath was haggard and forced. He kept trying to swallow, but could not close his mouth, so she continually wiped spittle and blood from his chin. It was painful to watch and caused tears to slide down Rachel's cheeks.

There had not been any love between her and Grant. Both had been forced into the marriage. He resented her for not being his wife of choice – he'd not really wanted a wife at all – and she had been bartered to him like a horse. But watching him lying there, struggling to hold on to his life, Rachel felt a deep remorse. Not an ambitious man, moody and angry at being tied down to a woman, Grant had mostly gone through the motions of being a husband. Still, he had come to her defense . . . and that single protective act was going to cost him his life.

13

'Dear Lord,' Rachel murmured a prayer. 'I'm sorry for the bad thoughts I've had about my husband. Please don't let him suffer for defending my honor.' She sniffed, not really knowing how to pray. Ever since she was old enough to attend Sunday meetings, she had been stuck with one or more babies to tend. She believed there was a God, but she had never been taught how to speak to Him properly. 'I'm sorry that I ain't been a better wife,' she concluded. 'Amen.'

There were Chinese work gangs all over California, up through New Mexico, Arizona, Colorado and even into Wyoming. Cantonese workers arrived on American shores, crowded on to a ship like cattle, then were bound to serve out indentures to whomever held their contract. For the immigrant laborers, it was the only way to get in to the country and start earning a living. Most of them hoped to earn more than enough for themselves, as many had families to support back in their homeland.

When times became hard and many people were out of work, it was easy to point the finger of blame at the Chinese: they kept to themselves, lived on dried squid, rice, tea and other dried vegetables and fish. They would also do any kind of work and usually cheaper than anyone else. There were demonstrations and even riots against the Chinese. Many people were angry they couldn't find work, yet the

Chinese all seemed to have jobs. And there were also some everyday bigots who didn't like them simply because they dressed and talked differently, had slanted eyes, and didn't readily blend in with the rest of society.

One of the few white men who befriended the Chinese was Phoenix Cline. He had once lived with Charlie Chong Lee and made many friends in the tight knit Chinese community. On leaving California, Phoenix had hired out his gun and earned a reputation for being quick and deadly in a fight. His last job in Surlock, Wyoming, had kindled his conscience and Phoenix returned to visit Charlie. He owed the man a great debt and had lately felt the need for the counsel and companionship of the Chinese savant.

As for Charlie, he had come to America back during the California gold rush of '49. For over a dozen years he had worked for the railroad and done any other jobs available. In his free time, he learned to read, write and speak excellent English. With a background in herbs and medicine from his homeland, Lee Chong eventually started his own business.

Charlie became something of a leader in the Chinese district of San Francisco. Understanding that Americans had difficulty comprehending the Chinese culture, he suggested the new arrivals invert their names to remove confusion and more closely match those in America. Hence, he became Chong Lee. To assimilate more easily, he added a first name of

Charlie. Charlie Chong Lee began educating and treating his countrymen and soon developed a thriving business that brought in customers of all races. His potions and gentle treatment of injuries became renown. Especially when many western doctors – most of whom had never been to medical school – knew little more than how to use leeches, do blood-letting and who would perform amputations for even minor bone breaks or infections. Men enjoyed his herbal and holistic approach to medicine; he was literate, displayed common sense and often quoted from Confucius or other literate men. Women, especially those who suffered cramps or recurrent headaches, saw him as a god-sent healer, a learned, eastern-hemisphere physician. Rather than selling them foul-smelling concoctions that tasted of alcohol or caster oil, he provided them with a ginseng potion that was pleasant tasting and relieved their pain. He was quick to recommend they use the potion sparingly, as the opium additive could cause the patient to become dependent on the drug.

Charlie had arrived on American shores a free man, but times had changed and the restrictions on Chinese immigration had grown stricter over the years until only the practice of indentures allowed new Chinese to get passage into the country. Charlie took it on himself to try to help those who paid their debts. He found work for many of them and contacted many others who could also help the free

Chinese find jobs. As such, Charlie was a popular man among those living in China Town.

It was a calm evening at Charlie's residence, where Phoenix Cline and he were passing the time, when trouble came calling. There had been several incidents of Chinese being attacked or beaten when they dared enter the main part of the city. There had also been an incursion or two from angry mobs, blaming the Chinese for the current level of high unemployment. This night, however, it was a local dispute which caused trouble to end up on Charlie's doorstep.

The unfortunate girl and her companion arrived only moments ahead of four men. Phoenix had been seated at a table with Charlie. By the time they stood up, the man was babbling wildly in his native tongue and the girl had thrown herself at Charlie's feet.

'What's going on, Charlie?' Phoenix asked, confused by the scene unfolding.

Charlie listened to a bit more of the other man's hasty chatter and then held up a hand to silence the panicked gent.

'It would seem, Baihu, that a vexing situation has arisen. Su Lee came to this country masquerading as a boy, but her secret is out.'

'So she's a girl, so what?'

Charlie's expression was grave. 'Two of the local tongs are claiming her. Each side wants her to go to work at one of their Joy Houses, so they might

17

sample her charms. Because of all the fuss, the overseer has discovered Su Lee is a girl. I'm sure they have their own idea about what she can do to earn money for him.'

'What kind of idea are you talking about?'

Charlie said. 'It is probable her owner will put her to work in a brothel somewhere. There is a shortage of Chinese girls in this country. She would be an exotic novelty, likely to be worth thousands of dollars to them.'

Phoenix looked down at the girl. She remained prostrate on the floor at Charlie's feet, her hat lost during their run, with her forehead placed right on top of his sandals. Her hair was in a single braid, but unlike the men, she had not shaved the front part of her head. She gasped for breath and wept with fear.

'What can you do for her?'

'She is indentured, Baihu. I can do nothing.'

The other Chinese looked over his shoulder and spied several men approaching the house. He cried something in his own language and ran to hide in one of the back rooms.

'What are our options here, Charlie?' Phoenix wanted to know. 'I'm not going to stand by and watch anyone be forced to work at a brothel.'

'The men approaching are not Chinese. I have no authority to do anything to prevent this from happening. I would be imprisoned or possibly hanged for opposing them.'

18

Phoenix knelt down at the girl's side, placed a hand beneath her chin and gently lifted her head up until he could look at her face. Terror glistened in her youthful eyes and tears wet her cheeks. She gave him an imploring look – a helpless fawn, awaiting death at the jaws of a wolf pack. The single expression inflamed Phoenix with a mixture of outrage and compassion.

'There are four of them,' Charlie warned. 'These are hard men, used to doing whatever they please. Only a fool would stand against such devils.'

Phoenix slid his hand to the girl's cheek and offered her a grim reassurance. 'You are safe with Charlie, little lady.' The words were gentle and calm. 'No one is going to harm you, not while I'm here.'

'Baihu, if you do this, there will be severe repercussions,' Charlie warned.

'Best start thinking of how to deal with them,' Phoenix told him quietly. 'I remember your quoting Confucius to me, something about, *To see right and not to do it is cowardice.*'

'I believe I also mentioned the one about, *When anger rises, think of the consequences.*'

'The consequences will be up to the men chasing this young lady,' Phoenix retorted. Then he stepped into the doorway and removed the thong from his gun. Indenture was one thing – slavery and forced prostitution was something else.

The four men had been running to catch up with

19

the girl and her escort. The group lumbered to an uncertain stop, seeing an armed white man stationed at the door. As Charlie had cautioned, each of the pursuers wore a gun and looked to have had experience in a fight. Phoenix wished he was wearing his dual holster rig. A second gun would have been handy, when facing four men. Too late to worry about it, he sized up the quartet with a glance. One man was darkly tanned and looked like he'd been in his share of scrapes – he would be dangerous. Two more were Mexican toughs, probably used as physical bullies. The last was fair of skin, with long, greasy brown hair. He stood in front of the others and looked to be the big-mouthed leader of the bunch.

'State your business, boys,' Phoenix invited, his voice masking the adrenaline surge which invaded his body. It caused an immediate prickling along his spine and every nerve seemed magnified and tensed for action.

'We've come for the Chink girl,' Big-mouth sneered.

'I find that term offensive, fella. What are you – Swede, Dutch, Irish, or just white mongrel trash?'

The man bridled, glowered at Phoenix and put a hand on the butt of his pistol. He was confident, having four to one odds. The two Mexicans showed wicked grins, whereas Dangerous appeared more wary. The dark-tanned man would be the quickest and most deadly of the four in a gunfight.

20

'I've got a paper here that shows I own that girl,' Big-mouth said importantly, patting his jacket pocket.

'Show me,' Phoenix said.

'I don't have to show you anything!' Big-mouth spat out the words. 'Get the hell out of our way . . . or we'll stomp you into the dust.'

'You'll find I'm not as easy to push around as the Chinese.'

'Look here,' Big-mouth snarled the words. 'The girl is legally ours and there's nothing you can do about it.'

'I can take her away from you,' Phoenix suggested easily.

'Oh, yeah?' was the man's clever retort.

'Question for you, mister. . . .' he leveled an icy stare at the man, 'Do you want to sell me this girl's indenture for a reasonable price, or do I get it for free when I take it off of your lifeless body?'

Big-mouth started to reply, but Dangerous put a hand on his arm to stop him. He was the one to ask, 'Just who are you, buster? And why are you taking the side of this here Chinese gal?'

'The name is Phoenix Cline,' he tossed out his name. 'And these people are friends of mine . . . including the young lady.'

Dangerous took a step back. 'Phoenix Cline,' he repeated the name as if it were hallowed. 'You're the man who tamed Waynesville and killed the Santa Fe

Kid in a street gunfight?'

'I'm the one.'

Dangerous looked at Big-mouth. 'Maybe you ought to name a price for the girl, Zack. I ain't looking to lock horns with Phoenix Cline.'

Big-mouth snorted his contempt. 'Fer hell sakes, he's only one man!'

'I'll give you two hundred dollars to sign over the girl's release,' Phoenix offered. 'That ought to be more than fair.'

But Big-mouth was not interested. 'She'll make more than that for me each and every night at one of the men's social clubs in town, Cline. Now, either you step aside or we'll walk over your dead body and take the girl. Choice is yours.'

Phoenix swept over the four men with a cool appraisal. He knew the time for talking had come to an end. Dangerous was obviously apprehensive about his speed with a gun, but the odds were heavily in their favor. Suddenly, like a man thinking he couldn't be killed, Big-mouth grabbed for his gun. Dangerous had been ready; he was already clearing leather—

Phoenix put a perfectly aimed round into the chest of Dangerous, then sprayed the other three . . . firing with extraordinary speed and marksmanship. Dangerous dropped like God had stuck him down from the sky with a big hammer. Big-mouth also took a bullet to the chest, hit hard enough that he lost his gun. He staggered to his knees as the other two targets were each stung by a lead missile from Phoenix's gun. Both of the Mexicans got off a single shot. One had panicked while hurrying his draw and fired right into the ground, while the bullet from the other missed Phoenix by two feet and sank into the wooden doorframe.

Poised, ready to expend his last round, Phoenix stood facing the four men. Dangerous lay dead and Big-mouth was close on his heels, mortally wounded. The two Mexicans each had wounds to their gun sides, one with a bloody shoulder and the other with a hole in his upper arm. Neither showed any interest in continuing the fight.

'I'll be taking that indenture,' Phoenix told Big-mouth, holstering his pistol and stepping forward. 'Doesn't look as if you'll be needing it any more.'

Big-mouth had one hand over the wound – the bullet had entered to the left of his sternum and pierced his lung – and his other was planted on the ground to keep himself upright. He rocked back on his heels and glared up at Phoenix. 'You stinkin' Chinaman lover,' he rasped.

'Yes, well, I obviously have a better taste in companions than you.'

'My brother . . .' he coughed up a mouthful of blood. 'You . . . you're dead, mister.'

'I've been dead before,' Phoenix told him dryly. Then he reached inside the man's jacket and

23

removed the indenture. As he glanced over the contract, Big-mouth slumped over on his side, coughed once more and died. The two wounded men uttered not a word, but left their guns in the dust and staggered away into the night to find a doctor.

'You have sealed my fate, young Baihu,' Charlie said from behind him. 'I must leave this city or my residence will become a local cemetery.'

Phoenix turned to look at him. The girl had gotten to her feet, stunned by what had happened and staring mouth agape. She regarded him with wide eyes of wonder and something else . . . gratitude.

'I'm the one who did the fighting, Charlie. I'll go clear this up with the chief of police. He isn't going to bring charges against me for stopping four men from forcing an innocent girl into prostitution.'

'The law doesn't affect the tongs, my son. They have their own rules of enforcement, and they have claimed Su Lee. It makes no difference that you were the victor in this fight, I will be killed for interfering with their business.'

'Then you'd best throw your things together. Looks like you'll be riding with me for a spell.'

'What about the indenture you forcibly extracted?'

Phoenix glanced at the paper again. 'Must be about a dozen names on this list.' The Chinese escort had reappeared from the back room, now that the

24

fight was over and, indicating the man, Phoenix said, 'Send your pal there to gather them. I'll visit the authorities, tend to the indenture, and clear my name over this little fracas. You pick up a wagon and some supplies. Better plan on us all leaving town in it as soon as I get back.'

Charlie uttered a sigh. 'I always knew you would one day darken my doorway and bring trouble.'

'What are friends for?' Phoenix asked with a grin.

CHAPTER TWO

Rachel stood rigid, arms folded, her posture displaying her ire and grim determination.

'I know how much this place means to you,' Don Baylor said carefully. 'But I don't want to see you get hurt. Hildebrand's men will keep pushing, and you're alone now. The dentist next door lost his place and the owner of the bath house up and moved away. You're all alone down here and certainly don't have enough business to hire any help. It's doubtful anyone would work for you under the circumstances anyway. With the Palace Saloon sitting on the corner of Main Street, your place is barely visible from the walkway. As for the railroad passengers, Hildebrand built a covered walk on the next block, so it leads customers directly to his Palace Inn. He's got you cut off from the rest of town. How do you expect to keep the business going all by yourself?'

'I don't have anywhere else to go,' she replied

curtly. 'My father-in-law is on his deathbed. His sister is living with him until he passes. I can't go stay with him, cause he don't have nothing left. We was supposed to help support him with the money we were going to make with this business. Now he's broke and dying, and my folks are poorer than a beggar's dog. They sold me off as a bride to be rid of me. I got no place to go back to.'

'Maybe you should take the money offered by Hildebrand?'

'I don't want no measly handout, just so it can ease his conscience!' Rachel hissed her reply, 'I'll die first!'

Baylor's shoulders sagged with the weight of defeat. 'I don't know what I can do, Mrs Pomeroy. Hildebrand owns the judge, the sheriff and those other two oafs who pose as deputies. He's got that massive ranch outside town and owns the Palace Saloon, the Silver Springs Pharmacy and the Palace Inn. When you look at the fact he has controlling interest in the bank and leases several other buildings in town, the guy is just too big and powerful to oppose.'

'I won't close my doors and give up,' Rachel vowed. 'If the bank forecloses on me, they'll have to drag me out of here.'

Baylor sighed. 'All right, Mrs Pomeroy. I can see that talking isn't going to do any good. And, to tell the truth, I understand your position. If I didn't have a wife and three kids, I'd be inclined to join you.'

'I ain't expecting no one to help,' Rachel said softly. 'I wouldn't ask you to get involved. I know you got a family to think of.'

'Even if I dared, I owe a fair-sized mortgage on my store. The pharmacy Hildebrand built carries a lot of the same merchandise as I do. They've undercut my prices on most of those things, so we're struggling to make ends meet.'

'Hildebrand moved in and wants to build himself an empire,' Rachel said thickly. 'And he don't care how many people he has to step on to get it.'

Baylor didn't argue the point. 'I wish you luck, Mrs Pomeroy. If there's anything I can do, you only have to ask.'

'Thank you, Mayor,' Rachel said. Then he left her at the walk and made the trek back up the street toward his store.

She stared after him and noticed he began to blur before her eyes. Only then did she realize tears had formed and were slipping down to wet her cheeks. She hadn't cried at Grant's funeral. She had just felt a great sense of isolation, not from losing Grant, but because she was left totally alone in her battle for survival. She would miss the security of having a man around, but she would not miss his sullen moods, nor the contempt in his voice when he complained of how he had been roped into a position he hated. The man had never treated her like a wife. She had been a chore, a burden, a cross he had to bear. Even when he touched her, she felt only anger and resentment, never affection. They had shared the business and their daily lives, but they had never shared even a tiny bit of love.

Rachel entered the café section and walked toward the kitchen. She would prepare chili con carne for anyone who stopped by for lunch. Chili or stew was about all she could afford to make and there were few customers – sometimes a freighter, a couple of cowboys or drifters. They chose her small eatery over the larger places because of the price – two bits for a bowl of chili or stew, along with a third of a loaf of bread and coffee to drink. She wondered how much longer she could afford to offer that much.

Zeke Lichen stood at the foot of the newly covered grave. He and Zack had been the only sons to Zeb Lichen and Mad Martha Granville. Although never married by a parson, Martha added Zeb's last name to the end of her own and the two of them stayed together for over twenty years. They had two boys and lived next to the Chinese district, where the kids grew up rowdy and enjoyed picking on their passive and usually submissive neighbors. Zeb had a job on the docks, while Martha worked at a nearby saloon. Between father and mother, they always managed to keep the boys fed and housed. Neither was around much for supervision or discipline of the pair, so the boys ran wild in their youth. They soon learned it was easy to get away with theft or robbery, so long as the victims were Chinese. Those people seldom contacted the law and, even if they did, the law usually ignored their complaints.

The years passed and Zeb had an accident and died several weeks later from the injuries. The boys were eighteen and twenty at the time. Martha had never been quite right but, while she had her looks, she earned money keeping lonely men company at the gambling tables and helping them drink up their money. Once her youth was lost, she became a cleaning woman at the saloon. That came to an end three years after Zeb's death, when she tried to roll a drunk. He woke up and stuck a knife into her chest, killing her instantly. Zeke and Zack handled that bit of retribution. The man died a horrific death, placed inside a coffin with several rattlesnakes and was buried alive.

The Lichen brothers continued their life of crime but, as time went on, they faced new dangers; the Chinese developed more unity and had an odd sort of brotherhood, organizations called tongs. And while they seldom risked anything against an outsider, they had a few enforcers among them. Growing weary of persecution, some of those in the 'fighting tong' dared to strike back against known thieves, regardless of race. Rather than risk that kind of trouble, Zack suggested buying a Contract of

Indenture and putting the Chinese to work for them.

Zeke went along with the idea, but found it was too much like work, searching out various jobs and then overseeing a labor gang for days or weeks at a time. He let Zack handle that end of things, while he started up a small gang of his own. They robbed stagecoaches, the occasional trading post, and a few travelers or payrolls. No longer restricted to Chinese victims, his crew stole whatever they could. It was profitable, and both boys had been making plenty of money.

Zeke reminisced about the good times in his mind, standing there at his brother's grave. Whether Zeb came home after too much drink and felt like beating his boys, or Martha suffered one of her mental lapses and ran through the streets naked, they had endured as a family. He and Zack had grown up wild and free and people quickly learned not to mess with the two Lichen boys. They were tough, brutal, and took no lip or insult from anyone. It had been a good life for him and Zack.

'You gonna' run that killer down?' A voice of one of his gang, Chips Longmont, asked gently.

'You and the others don't have to trail along,' Zeke replied. 'This is personal.'

'We ain't got nothing else going on, Zeke. Ivan and Stummer are willing and I've already saddled my horse.'

'The man not only murdered my little brother, he

31

ran off with Zack's whole Chinese work crew. They've got a two day head start. It might take us a month to track them down.'

Chips shrugged. 'Like I said, Zeke, we've got nothing else to do.'

'Then pick up supplies for a hard ride. A man like Phoenix Cline shouldn't be hard to find.'

'Yeah, especially riding with a dozen coolies.'

Zeke uttered a sigh. 'I'm the last of the Lichen family. My ma and pa are dead. Now my baby brother is underground.'

'We'll make Phoenix die hard, same as you and Zack did with that skunk who killed your ma.'

Zeke blinked back his tears and patted Chips on the shoulder. 'You're right. We'll make that two-bit gunnie wish he'd never been born.'

Several days on the train and another week on the trail by wagon had put San Francisco a thousand miles behind them. Riding cross-country between railroad stops, Phoenix continued to look for something. He wasn't sure what he was searching for, but knew he would recognize it when he found it.

'What are your plans for the future, my young friend?' Charlie asked, obviously curious about their destination. 'We have passed through several states and territories, and you have said little of your plans.'

'I'm looking for the right place to start over, Charlie.'

'You have acquired a most unusual wealth, the accumulation of human laborers.'

'That wasn't my intention at the time.'

'The result is what counts. You hold the indenture of a dozen workers. How will they pay you their debt?'

'Look, I only gave a hundred dollars to the police chief. He was going to take care of the indenture for me. As for these people, they don't owe me anything.'

'I tried to tell as much to the senior member of the group, Fang Chow. However, he insisted that he and the others are bound by their honor to pay off the one year contract. They still owe six more months of service.'

Phoenix groaned. 'I only wanted to help the girl.'

'My niece is very thankful . . . as am I.'

'Your niece?' Phoenix's head snapped around and he stared at the man. 'All this time we've been together and now you tell me Su Lee is your niece!'

'I neglected to mention it, until such time as it was no longer relevant to our situation. It would have been self-serving of me to tell you when she and Fang Chow fled to my house. I didn't want you taking on a fight that was not your own. I knew if you were aware that she was family, you would have involved yourself on my account.'

'Well, hell yeah, I'd have involved myself! I owe you my life. You should have said something.'

A fatherly expression settled on Charlie's face. 'It was unnecessary, you did the noble deed without knowing the truth.' He uttered a sigh and changed the direction of the conversation.

'I came to America as a young man. I have no other family here. It would do my heart good to see Su Lee wed a fine and proper young man. As you have saved her from the degradation of serving in a Joy House, I am obliged to offer her to you first.'

Phoenix laughed. 'When it comes to fine and proper, I don't exactly fit the mould. I thank you, but the young lady deserves a whole lot better than me.'

'She is a beautiful girl,' Charlie persisted.

'Yes, and one who should try to find a man she can love, not marry out of obligation for a debt that doesn't exist.'

'Then you relinquish any claim on her, Baihu?'

'You help find her a suitable man, one who will make her happy. That's the claim I relinquish to you.'

Charlie smiled his relief. 'And what about your plans for the future?'

'I expect I'll have to keep an eye out for the brother of the one man I killed. He mentioned he would get revenge with his dying breath.'

'Yes, I heard the threat. Also, the infamy and evil ways of the two Lichen brothers are well known throughout the Chinese district.'

'Zeke and Zack Lichen,' Phoenix spoke of the two

34

men. 'The police chief thanked me for killing Zack and wished me luck with Zeke. I got the impression he would like to be rid of both of them.'

'When you went to confess about the gunfight, I was apprehensive they might lock you away in a cell.'

'Four men against one, and me defending the honor of a young lady?' Phoenix uttered a mirthless laugh. 'No way they were going to charge me on something like that.'

'Yes, but she was Chinese.'

Phoenix rubbed his chin with his free hand. 'Don't recall her heritage coming into the conversation. It shouldn't matter one way or the other.'

'He must have guessed when you produced the indenture papers.'

Phoenix laughed. 'Like you said, the authorities are probably aware that Zack and his brother are both outlaws.'

Charlie let the matter drop. 'You told me you had changed since your last job, that you no longer wanted to sell your gun and troubleshoot for other people. So you have begun this quest by killing two men.'

'That's not fair,' Phoenix said. 'I gave the man a choice. He could have sold me the girl. I still intend to do something I can be proud of – make a difference.'

Charlie smiled. 'Perhaps I and this group of indentured workers can help with your endeavors. Do you have a task in mind, Baihu?'

Phoenix had learned a little about Chinese folk-lore from having been in Charlie's care for several months. During his recovery – and subsequent renaming – Charlie had often espoused his philosophy about the meaning of life. He dubbed Phoenix *Baihu*, meaning White Tiger, because he had fought overwhelming odds and survived. For his new life, Phoenix assumed the name of a mythical bird, which he thought was more appropriate, having come back from the dead. Charlie had teased him about it, considering the Phoenix is fabled in Chinese lore to be a Yin or *fenghuang*, which is the female counterpart to the male Yang, or a dragon.

He didn't comment to Charlie about the nickname of Baihu. Instead, he outlined his vision. 'I recently passed through a number of towns that are sprouting up along the railroad line. It's why we've come all the way to Colorado. I think we can find a place to set up shop somewhere in these parts.'

'Then you envision a business venture of some sort?'

'That's right, Charlie. I aim to find a place where you and these other folks can put down roots and start earning a living. Once everyone is satisfied that the indenture is paid, I intend for you to all have businesses of your own.'

'A most worthwhile project, Baihu. I'm sure the others will be pleased with the idea.' He said the words of praise, but he was also reserved. 'Of course, you are aware that some towns are not fond of adding Chinese to their populace. There are many who resent our ways.'

'That's why we'll pick a town that's in the middle of the growing process. Then if someone doesn't like it, I can explain it to them.' Phoenix grinned. 'Everyone knows I'm a reasonable person.'

'I saw your reasoning first hand our last night in San Francisco.'

Phoenix chuckled. 'It's a last resort, my good friend. It pays to be prepared.'

The smile widened. 'Confucius once said: *never give a sword to a man who can't dance.*'

Phoenix frowned. 'What the devil does that mean?'

Charlie laughed. 'I surmise it refers to an unusual style of dancing.'

Rachel clenched her fists and glared at Nape. His deputy's badge was crooked – significant in that it matched his character. He had just driven away a couple of wandering cowboys who were looking for a place to spend the night.

'You've no right stopping customers from coming to my place for lodging,' she stated testily. 'I'm not doing no one any harm.'

'Aw, Rachel, honey,' he slurred the words. 'You know how this is going to end. Mr Hildebrand done offered you a fair price . . . and he is willing to let you work for him. I don't know what more you could want.'

'I ain't gonna' work for him, and I ain't gonna' let him drive me out of my business either!'

Nape laughed at her stubbornness. 'Look at the facts, Rachel, honey. You've been a widow for over a month and you haven't had but a handful of customers. Jimmy, over at the bank, told me your mortgage is due at the end of next month. How you going to pay him?'

'I'll find a way,' she maintained her stance. 'You and the rest of your bully pals don't own the world. I'll send word to the US Marshal about how you are preventing people from staying or eating at my place. I'll tell him how you killed my husband and drove off our help.'

'The US Marshal wouldn't make the trip all the way from Denver just to look into your complaint.' He snickered, 'Especially when you can't even pay your bills.'

A team and wagon turned from the main street and appeared headed toward the boarding-house. Rachel could make out several Chinese and a white man. She was surprised they were coming her way, but if they needed meals or rooms, she would gladly accept their business.

'Why are you doing this?' she asked Nape, keeping his attention on her rather than the approaching

38

wagon. She knew he would likely send them away, so she tried to reason with the deputy. 'A few customers won't make all that much difference.'

But Nape was done being civil. He grabbed hold of her arms and glared at her. His fingers gripped the flesh until Rachel gasped from the pain. She began to struggle, aware that the wagon had stopped a short distance away.

'You best get off of the high horse you're riding, Rachel, honey. You start being nice to me and maybe I'll allow one or two drifters to eat here or rent rooms from you.'

'You're hurting me!' she cried, twisting in his grasp. 'Let go!'

He braced his feet and muscled her to a standstill. 'I've a mind to take some of the fire out of you, you hot-tempered little witch. Maybe Blocker was right. After being married to a no-account weakling, I'd wager you're like a mustang what needs to be broke-to-ride by a real man.'

Without warning, the barrel of a gun struck Nape above the temple. His face went suddenly lax, his eyes turned glassy and he dropped like a sack of grain. As his hold was broken, Rachel stepped back, stunned that the new arrival had slipped up behind Nape and clouted him with his gun. With her mind reeling, she stood agog, while her rescuer rolled Nape off of the porch with the toe of his boot.

'Pardon the interruption, ma'am.' The rather

handsome man spoke nonchalantly, as if he had simply shooed away an unwanted dog. 'I spoke to the gent over at the general store and he said your boarding-house might have room for me and my friends.' He hooked a thumb to indicate the dozen or so Chinese in the wagon.

'I . . .' she had to swallow to catch her breath and get her voice to work. She cast a quick look at Nape. He groaned, but was still incoherent, facedown on the dusty street. 'You bet, mister. I ain't got no guests staying here at the moment.'

'I tried the big hotel on main street, but they have a sign out front which reads: *No Dogs, Indians or Chinese*,' he explained. 'That's when I spoke to the guy at the store. I promise you, these are the most courteous, well mannered customers you could hope for.'

'I'd be happy to have all of you stay, but Nape is. . . .' she pointed at the stunned man. 'He's a deputy sheriff,' she explained. 'Hitting him like you done, I expect you're going to end up sleeping behind bars, instead of at my place.'

He showed not the slightest concern. 'Deputy sheriff, huh?'

'Yes.'

'Not to worry,' he waved the notion aside. 'Charlie will take care of his flock until I sort out my situation with the local law.' Turning he cocked his head toward the group. 'Charlie's the elderly gent just climbing down from the wagon.'

'And you?'

'Name's Phoenix Cline. I kind of got stuck riding herd over some of Charlie's friends. We need a place for a few days, until I can find something permanent.'

'If you've got money, you're welcome to stay here as long as you like.'

The man he had called Charlie walked up to them. He glanced at Nape, gave a resigned shake of his head and sighed. 'Confucius says: *a superior man is modest in his speech, but exceeds in his actions.*'

Phoenix grinned. 'That's me, a man of few words.'

'I have eight rooms,' Rachel informed the two men. 'There are two beds in each room. There's also a corral out back for your horses. I don't have any feed on hand, but. . . .'

'We'll pick up some later at the livery,' Phoenix said. He turned to Charlie. 'If the men double-up, Su Lee and I can each have our own room.'

'We shall arrange it to be so, Baihu.'

'If you need more space, I have a second bed in my room,' Rachel volunteered. 'The young lady can share with me.'

'You're benevolent and supremely accommodating, but that arrangement will be unnecessary,' Charlie said politely. 'We are honored to share your dwelling and will be quite comfortable without imposing on your generosity.'

Rachel lifted her brows in wonder. 'You talk the best English of any man I ever met.'

He performed a humble bow and replied, 'In a foreign land, a proper education is not optional, it is a necessity.'

Nape grunted as his brain began to function. He rolled on to his back, wiped at the dirt on his face and struggled to a sitting position. Recouping his bearings, he glared up at Phoenix.

'What the hell, mister?' he snarled the words.

'You don't want to be mistreating a lady when I'm around.'

Nape curled his legs under him and rose unsteadily to his feet. He paused to rub the tender lump on the side of his head. 'You just stepped in it with both feet, bud. I'll be back with the sheriff.'

'Good idea. I'd like to have a talk with him,' Phoenix replied easily. 'I'll be here when you get back.'

Nape cursed the new arrival's gall under his breath and lumbered away, staggering every few steps, as his normal balance was not yet fully intact.

'He means it; he'll bring back the sheriff,' Rachel cautioned.

Phoenix dismissed her warning. 'Could you direct me to the town's mayor?'

'Don Baylor is the man you want. You probably done talked to him already. He runs the general store.'

'Yes, we met, but he didn't mention he was mayor of Silver Springs.'

'It ain't like he has any real authority or nothing,' she informed him. 'Still and all, he's a good, honest man.'

'I perceive my literary teachings may be of some benefit here in Silver Springs,' Charlie interceded wryly. 'I believe this thriving metropolis has yet to implement an institution for educating the local populace in proper grammar and speech.'

Phoenix smirked. 'Yeah, it could use a school too.'

'Ah, Baihu, you are a master of the obvious.'

'Charlie, ask a couple of the boys to put away the team and my horse, once they are settled in. You and I should go over and pick up some supplies. I doubt the lady keeps a lot of dried fish and rice on hand.'

'Am I to presume we are staying here for a time?'

'We'll see what our conversation with the mayor yields,' Phoenix evaded.

Charlie spoke in Chinese to the people in the wagon, then turned to Rachel. 'If you would show my friends to their rooms, they will get situated and put away their belongings. Su Lee and Fang Chow speak some English. I have been working with the others during our travels, but none are yet fluent in the language.'

Rachel bobbed her head. 'All right, I'll see they get settled in.'

Phoenix tipped his hat to her and then left with

43

Charlie at his side. As the two of them walked toward the general store, she found herself surrounded by several of the Chinese. She offered a smile of greeting, but got back only curious stares. She noticed the girl was as dusty and dirty as the rest. They had obviously been traveling for a long time.

'I'll show you the rooms and where you can clean up,' she told them. At the blank looks returned, she wondered how much English any of them actually knew. Deciding it didn't matter – these were paying guests – she led the way into the boarding-house.

CHAPTER THREE

When Nape Cod entered the sheriff's office, Ponce Martell had been sitting with his feet on the desk. He quickly sat up straight when he saw Nape holding a hand up to a dark welt on the side of his head and asked, 'What happened to you?'

Nape's voice was thick with ire. 'Some drifter clipped me with his gun barrel, Martell. He sneaked up from behind and I never seen it coming.'

'Where did this happen?'

'I was down watching the widow's boarding-house, making sure she didn't get any customers – the way you told me.'

'And this guy took exception to your running him off?'

Nape shuffled his feet and did not meet the sheriff's incredulous look. 'Uh, not exactly.'

'So what happened?'

Nape gave his head a tilt to one side. 'You know

45

how it is,' he lamented. 'I was trying to talk sense to the widow. I figured I would straighten her out on her situation.'

The light of understanding flooded Martell's features. 'Oh, that's just fine. Some jasper caught you manhandling Mrs Pomeroy and knocked you into a cocked hat!'

Nape lowered his head like a scolded child. 'I wasn't doing her any harm.'

'Who was it? Do you know who hit you?'

'I was kind of woozy when I woke up, so I didn't try and tackle him alone.' Nape fingered the sore spot. 'He's a stranger, and I think he must be the boss over a bunch of Chinamen,' he said, recalling the men he had seen with his attacker,' 'cause he had a wagon full of them.'

'Probably an indentured work gang. You see them all the time along the railroad. Wonder why he went to the Pomeroy House?'

'It's got me stumped.'

'You get stumped trying to decide between using a knife or fork,' Martell jeered. 'Go wake up Blocker. The three of us will go down and parley with this troublemaker . . . before we toss him in a cell and teach him a lesson.'

'I aim to get even with that guy,' Nape vowed. 'Dirty skunk hit me from behind.'

Martell waved a hand in a flippant motion. 'Yeah, I hear you. Now go get Blocker. He had the night watch and is probably asleep in his bunk. This guy won't be so tough against three of us.'

Nape hurried out the door and Martell went to the gun rack. He chose the double-barrel, twelve-gage shotgun from the row of guns. He broke it open, shoved a load of buckshot into either chamber, while wondering who the interfering attacker was. A good many men, seeing Nape getting rough with a woman, might have stepped up to defend her. But this was a stranger with a Chinese work gang. What could he want in Silver Springs?

Snapping the gun closed, he walked over to the window so he could keep watch for Nape and Blocker. Soon as they arrived, the three of them would get to the bottom of the mysteries surrounding the newcomer.

Saving the nicest room, the one overlooking the street, for Phoenix, Rachel showed the group of men and the one lone girl to the other rooms.

'We have a bath downstairs,' she told the girl. 'You understand? A bath?'

Su displayed a puzzled frown.

Rachel imitated the act of washing her face and hands. 'Wash? Bath? Understand?'

A light of comprehension sprang into the girl's eyes and a smile appeared on her lips. 'Wash . . . yes.' Su bowed her thanks.

Rachel left them sorting out who would stay

where, and quickly checked the bedroom she had picked for Phoenix. While straightening the curtains, she caught sight of three men approaching from the main part of town. She recognized them at once – Martell and his two deputies. She rushed out of the room, her heart pounding with a dread anticipation. Then she went down the stairs and hurried toward the front of the building. Phoenix seemed a most capable man, but there were three of the bully lawmen. What chance would he have against such odds?

Fortunately, by the time Rachel arrived at the boarding-house entrance, she spied Phoenix and Charlie, who was carrying a sack of supplies, also heading her way. With the general store closer than the sheriff's office, they arrived a few steps ahead of the lawmen.

Phoenix spoke to Charlie, as they reached the porch, and told him to take their purchase inside. He turned about to face the three lawmen who were but a short distance away.

'Ponce Martell, the one in the middle, is the sheriff,' Rachel informed him, standing at his side. 'That there burly brute killed my husband several weeks back. He beat him so badly with his fists that he died a coupla days afterwards.'

'Your husband must have been a sizeable gent to tackle a man as big as him.'

'Uh-uh, he wasn't near as big as you. He was just

48

trying to protect me. Blocker pulled me down on his lap and was trying to kiss me. He only done it to force Grant into a fight so he would have an excuse to kill him.'

That was as much as she had time to say. The three men arrived and spread out a few feet apart, poised and ready for a fight.

'I'm Sheriff Martell,' the paunchy lawman in the middle spouted importantly, brandishing the shotgun menacingly. 'Nape tells me you sneaked up behind him and hit him with your gun . . . knocked him senseless, you did.'

Phoenix once more wished he was wearing two guns. He gave Rachel a slight push, so she would not be standing next to him. Once she was out of the line of fire, he squared his stance to face the three men.

'Nape wasn't showing much sense to start with, Martell,' Phoenix replied. 'He was accosting the lady. As for you, what business is it of yours?'

'I told you, I'm the sheriff of Silver Springs!'

Phoenix gave his head a negative shake. 'You're mistaken on that point, Martell. You were never sworn in to the position of Sheriff.'

The declaration stunned Martell. 'What are you talking about?'

'The mayor informed me that he didn't appoint you to the office, and there was never an official election. By whose authority did you pin on the badge and call yourself sheriff?'

Martell's face reddened, flustered at the nerve of this popinjay. 'I don't know where you think you're going with this. I was appointed to my office by Thurmond Hildebrand.'

'And what civil authority does he have?'

'He's the richest, most powerful man in the country.'

Phoenix laughed with disdain. 'I see, might makes right. He's one of those who lives by the golden rule . . . man with the most gold makes the rules.'

'Yeah, you could say that.'

'Well, I'm sorry, Martell, but I don't acknowledge you as being a representative of the law, and neither would a proper judge. At best, you are a municipal regulator or private police force empowered by a single wealthy gent who thinks he runs this town.'

'Look, you!' Martell snarled. 'I'm the law and you attacked one of my deputies. Now you're going to jail for that!'

Phoenix let his right hand rest on the butt of his pistol. 'Your deputy was molesting a young lady.' He gave a slight nod toward Rachel. 'And I'm told that the other ugly mutt with you murdered her husband a short time back.'

'Hey! that was a fair fight!' Blocker shouted. 'He even threw the first punch.'

'And what did you do to force him to fight? Tried to grope and kiss his wife, didn't you?' Phoenix surveyed the three men with a frosty stare. 'You're a fraud, Martell, and your two deputies are women molesters and bullies, a pair of maggots who should be behind bars, not wearing a badge.'

'Enough!' Martell snapped. 'We're going to put your name on a tombstone.'

'I've already seen my name on a tombstone,' Phoenix retorted frankly. 'After I was dead and buried I took on the handle of Phoenix Cline.'

Martell's eyes widened in shock. He dropped the shotgun, as if it had suddenly burned his hands. He took an involuntary step backward, his mouth worked, but no words came out.

'Phoenix Cline!' Nape exclaimed, lifting his hands well away from his gun. 'Holy, jumpin' Hannah!'

Blocker threw a blank stare at his two pals, like a horse suddenly lost without the guidance of a rider. 'Who is Phoenix Cline?' he asked.

Nape's head swiveled back and forth on his shoulders. He frowned at Blocker as if he was the dumbest man on earth. 'He's the most deadly man with a gun who ever lived!'

'Now I've spoken to the mayor,' Phoenix ignored the chatter between the two deputies and directed his words at Martell. 'He said, for the time being, you can continue to act in the capacity of sheriff. But only so long as you uphold the law and don't try and use the position to intimidate people ... like Mrs Pomeroy here.'

'Uh, yeah, that sounds fair,' Martell muttered,

51

finally able to find his voice.

'Of course, you'll have to arrest Blocker for killing Grant Pomeroy. He'll have to go before a judge for that crime.'

Martell's face blanched at the order, but he gave his head an affirmative nod.

'As far as your other deputy is concerned, if he attempts to put his hands on another woman. . . .' He bore into Nape with a deadly gaze, 'I'll take them away from him.'

Nape frowned in befuddlement. 'How you going to take away my hands?'

Phoenix regarded him with a mirthless smile. 'I'll bury them under six feet of dirt. You can choose whether or not they are still attached to your body!'

Nape gave a fleeting glance at his hands, swallowed hard, and began to back away. Blocker didn't understand what was going on, but he also started to move backward.

'You're not thinking about staying in Silver Springs?' Martell managed the question in a rather squeaky voice.

'I'll be here long enough to see your deputy stand trial for murder,' Phoenix replied.

Martell still had a sickly pallor. He bent at the middle, groaning from the effort, and picked up the shotgun. Once in hand, he swung around and started to walk away.

'I mean it, Sheriff,' Phoenix's words followed the

man. 'Blocker stands trial, or I'll be forced to deal out my own judgment.'

Martell didn't look back, but his head moved up and down at the warning. Then the trio was hurrying up the street, heading back to the main part of town.

Phoenix watched them go, wondering how long he could stick around town without exposing his back to a bullet. Those three would be trouble. And, according to the mayor, the bull of the country, Thurmond Hildebrand, was rich, powerful and greedy. He wanted the Pomeroy House so he could build a loading dock for the railroad. It was in the perfect location for what he wanted, except the lady refused to sell.

'Who are you?' a feminine voice asked at his side.

Phoenix turned to discover Rachel Pomeroy had not moved from the porch and was eying him with unmasked curiosity. She was well proportioned and had pleasant features. Her rich black hair, though pulled back in a style he had heard termed as a *pony-tail*, added an intrinsic beauty to her dark blue eyes. Slender, sensuous lips, modest brows and thick eyelashes, with skin as soft as a baby's cheeks . . . yes, *pleasant* was a good description.

'You must have heard me introduce myself,' he said.

'I don't mean your name,' she remarked. 'But it seems Martell and his dimwit deputies – one of them at least – has heard of you. How come?'

'Phoenix is a gem among men,' Charlie intervened, having watched the confrontation from inside the boarding-house door. He joined them on the porch.

Phoenix laughed. 'Go ahead, Charlie, tell her what Confucius would say about me.'

'*Better a diamond with a flaw than a pebble without,*' he offered. 'Phoenix Cline is a man to step aside for. His notoriety is widespread.'

'Noto . . . what?' Rachel wanted to know.

'His reputation,' Charlie clarified. 'It is said of Phoenix Cline's prowess with a gun, that only God's hand is quicker or more deadly.'

Phoenix laughed, at the absurd description. 'See to putting together a meal for your family and getting everyone settled,' he told Charlie. 'The lady and I have some palavering to do.'

'Very good, my friend. I shall speak with you later.'

Phoenix waited until Charlie had left. Then he faced Rachel with a solemn expression.

'Mrs Pomeroy, I have a proposition for you.'

She made a face. 'A proposition? You ain't asking me to marry you?'

He relaxed and a smile played on his lips. 'I admit the idea isn't totally uninviting, but I had more of a business proposition in mind.'

Race Killroke was waiting at the sheriff's office for Martell. Race was Thurmond Hildebrand's ramrod, hired gun, enforcer, and most any other title which suited him. When there was trouble of any kind, Race was the man to deal with it. Before the sheriff had time to put away his shotgun, Race made the reason for his visit known.

'Martell, the boss thinks we ought to increase the local taxes another per cent. We're going into the hole each month from keeping so many people on the payroll.'

The sheriff growled. 'He might not have to worry about that much longer, not if the guy who just squatted at the Pomeroy House sticks around. He clubbed Nape alongside the head, then threatened me and the boys. I'm to put Blocker in jail so he can stand trial for murder.'

Race sputtered in confusion. 'What are you talking about?'

'The man arrived with a pack of Chinese – don't know what that's about – but you've probably heard of him. Phoenix Cline.'

The news struck Race like a punch to the gut. He suddenly lost too much wind to form any words. After a few seconds, he composed himself and began to pace the office.

'Phoenix Cline, here in Silver Springs.' He pinned Martell with a sharp gaze. 'Do you know who hired him or who he's after?'

'I don't know that he was hired or came here looking for anyone. He spoke to Baylor and claims I wasn't properly appointed or elected.'

'He said that?'

'Yep, says I'm not legally a sheriff, though he'll allow I can continue to wear the badge . . . so long as I follow the letter of the law.'

'Who does the guy think he is, the governor of the state?'

Nape spoke up. 'Tell you what he ain't, Killroke, he ain't someone I'm going up against with a gun. That man is death on the hoof, pure lightning in a bottle. I wouldn't draw against him with five men at my side.'

'Nobody is that fast.'

'He killed the Santa Fe Kid in a main street shootout a year or so back,' Nape argued. 'I talked to the stage driver who seen it. Everyone thought the Kid was quicker than a ray of sunlight. Well, he never even cleared leather . . . and he had first go!'

'A bullet in the back don't care how fast you are.'

'Well, I ain't going to be the one to try,' Nape maintained. 'Nope. Martell can have my badge first. There ain't enough money in the country for me to try and take out Phoenix Cline.'

'What brought about this little confrontation?' Race asked Martell.

Martell began with how Nape had been turning away customers and ended with the encounter and warning at the porch.

'And the gunman arrived with a passel of Chinese?'

'That's right. Don't know how many, but Nape said the wagon was full of them.'

Race wondered aloud, 'What is he doing with a bunch of coolies?'

'One thing's certain, he's staying at the Pomeroy House,' Martell said. 'With a bunch of paying customers, it's going to make Mrs Pomeroy impossible to break.'

Race swore. 'That's something we don't need.'

'Yes, well, I'm going along with what Nape said; we ain't getting paid enough to risk our necks against the likes of Phoenix Cline.'

'You mean you're going to put Blocker in jail?'

Martell swallowed his consternation long enough to wink at Race. 'It's OK. We'll have Judge Eaton rule on the case. He can find Blocker guilty of too much force – something like that and slap him with 30 days of community service.'

'Sounds like a good idea, though you'd better set it up for tomorrow. You don't want to give Phoenix time to wire for a circuit judge.'

'I'll speak to Eaton this afternoon,' Martell promised. Then returned back to the other puzzle. 'What about the Chinese? I can't figure why a man like Phoenix would be traveling with them. You think he might be going around hiring out workers?'

Race hunched his shoulders in a shrug. 'Don't ask me. I'll speak to the boss when I get back out to the house. We still need Pomeroy's property.'

'Rachel might still default on her loan. Jimmy Lyndon told me she has only a few weeks left. If he can foreclose on it, Hildebrand might still get it.'

'That's what we've been counting on,' Race said. 'I'll head on back to the ranch and tell the boss about Phoenix Cline and the Chinese and also about Blocker going on trial for murder. He's not going to be happy about any of this.'

Martell stood to one side so Race could leave. 'Tell him we'll get the judge to go easy on Blocker beating up Grant. Don't see any reason for Mr Hildebrand to have to come in for the hearing, not unless the judge balks about it for some reason.'

'Eaton is on the payroll and a worthless drunk,' Race said. 'He'll do what he's told . . . unless he wants the whiskey well to dry up.'

'I'll remind him,' Martell promised. 'I'm sure he'll go along.'

Race went out of the room and Martell pointed his finger at Blocker. 'You best stay here at the jail until we get this thing settled. No need giving Phoenix an excuse to shoot you down on the street.'

Blocker didn't argue. 'A cot in the cell sounds a whole bunch better than a bullet in the gut.'

Rachel sat in bewilderment. She had listened quietly, while Phoenix outlined his plan. When he'd finished, her sky blue eyes were fixed on him – filled with curiosity, disbelief, and something else . . . suspicion?

'Why would you do something like this?' she asked, breaking the interminable silence that had gripped the room since he had finished.

'For Charlie and the others.'

'Yes, but there are lots of places where you could do that, without risking your life against a bunch of crooked lawmen and a man as powerful as Thurmond Hildebrand.'

'Listen to me, Mrs Pomeroy. There are Chinese restaurants doing business in nearly every major city or town across the country. And no one can compete with them on prices when it comes to laundry. Plus, Charlie is a pharmacist and physician. A lot of people will come to him for his doctoring skills.'

'So your idea is to use the storage room next to the kitchen and make the eating part bigger. Then your Chinese friends will open a big laundry where the bath house used to be, and Charlie will use the place where Mr Williams had his dentist office.'

'The dining area ought to be big enough to hold at least thirty people,' Phoenix suggested. 'And it won't be any problem to add a laundry setup to the bath house. The water heaters and tubs are already there. We only have to add a counter and bins for doing business. As for Charlie, he will open a practice for medicine, and he can use the back of the office for his living quarters and patients or holding class.'

'Class?'

'He is a skilled teacher. Anyone who wants to learn to read and write can enroll for a small fee.' Phoenix continued with his proposal. 'Don't you see? This will not only allow you to keep this place, but it'll be much bigger and make a lot more money. You're the owner of all the property. You'll get a percentage from the restaurant, laundry, and everything Charlie and the Chinese take in.'

'Why should I get anything from the laundry or Charlie's doctoring?'

'Because you would be my partner. So long as they owe me for their indenture, they owe you too. Once the debt is paid, they will pay rent for the property.'

Rachel did some thinking before asking, 'What would my job be?'

'About what you've been doing. You can run the boarding-house and help cook meals – we'll serve both regular and Chinese food. Once Su Lee and the others learn enough English, they can help with whatever is needed and you'll be the boss.'

'With you and the others, the boarding-house is full.'

'Not for long,' Phoenix informed her. 'The Chinese are a private people and prefer their own dwellings. It won't take long before they build huts or set up tents out back. Then you'll have the rooms back.' He added, 'Except for mine, of course.'

'What do you get out of this?'

'Room and board, along with a percentage until

the indenture is paid. After that, I'll have a share of your place until you buy me out.'

Her skepticism lingered. 'I don't believe you're doing this for the money.'

'I owe Charlie my life. This is a way to repay him. Plus I will also earn a percentage of the profits for putting up the money for the remodel and any additional things we need.'

Rachel was again thoughtful. 'I don't know about being partners.'

'It's like I told you. Any time you wish to buy me out, the price will be exactly the amount of money I use to transform this place.'

The girl studied him closely, as if trying to see if this was some kind of con. 'I'd like to trust you, but. . . .'

'I'll sign a written contract if you like.'

'I . . . I ain't able to read,' she admitted. 'I know a few words, like "stew" or "chili", but not much more. I am good with numbers though. I can make change and add up totals and enter them in a ledger. Grant learned me to do that much.'

'Charlie can teach you to read and write. He's very gifted.'

Rachel's eyes again bore into him with a level stare. Her question was blunt. 'You didn't answer my first question. Why did you choose me and my place?'

'You might be in financial trouble, but you have a

61

good location. We'll get a lot of traffic from the train. Since the laying of tracks, there are small eateries at every fuel or rest stop. During those periods, people hurry to those nearby places to buy meals. A good many little diners earn their living serving passengers. As far as the Chinese food goes, it's becoming real popular around the country. We'll have people coming from miles around to try it.'

'Hildebrand put in a wooden walkway to his restaurant, so the people getting off of the train would go to his place.'

'We'll put up a sign with an arrow pointing this way, or we might have one of the Chinese meet the train and inform the passengers of your place. They could hand out menus listing the meals and prices. That way, even if the folks went to Hildebrand's place first, they would discover the Pomeroy House is much cheaper.'

The woman remained cautious and curious. 'You could have gone anywhere to start up your business. There are a number of towns being built along the railroad. I still have to wonder, why here and why me?'

'Would you believe I've been looking for a special kind of partner?' At her curious mien, he continued. 'She has to be a newly widowed proprietor, desperate to save her place, yet one who is beautiful, with raven-black hair and sparkling blue eyes.' He grinned. 'No telling how many towns I would have to check along the route before I found another partner like you.'

'Sparkling blue eyes?'

He smiled. 'Yes, the prettiest eyes I've ever seen.'

Rachel smiled at his humor. 'I ain't never been romanced before . . . not properly. Are you flirting with me?'

'Let's just say I was making a backdoor sort of compliment.'

She grew serious again. 'Tell me more about how you're going to get all of this done . . . and when do we start making money. The bank note is due the end of next month. If I don't pay it, the bank will take my place. It don't give us much time.'

'I'll take care of the note,' he promised. 'For the past few years I've earned high wages and cash bounties on some of the men I've helped put away. We'll buy what we need and we've plenty of help. We should have things up and running in no time.'

'It sounds too good to be true.'

'I promise, this is on the level.' She didn't say anything more, so he presented the question: 'What's your answer to my proposition? Are we partners?'

Rachel put forth her hand. 'Yes, Mr Cline. Partners.'

CHAPTER FOUR

Thurmond sat back in his leather-bound chair, placed both hands on to the desktop and gazed at Race in disbelief. 'Phoenix Cline, the famous gunman, in Silver Springs?'

'That's right, boss. He arrived with a bunch of Chinese and has settled in at the Pomeroy House.'

The man groaned. 'I can't believe it. Of all the towns in the country, and all of the boarding-houses in those towns, why in blazes did he have to choose my town and the Pomeroy House!'

'He also demanded that Blocker Quade stand trial for killing Grant Pomeroy.'

Thurmond groaned. 'Somehow, that doesn't surprise me.'

'Next he talked to the mayor and challenged the actual authority Martell and his boys have ... seeing's how they weren't elected or appointed properly.'

'The man has certainly been busy! I should have stripped Baylor of his position as mayor. I was afraid something like this might come back to haunt me.'

'Martell is going to have Judge Eaton rule on Blocker's case. Figure Blocker can do a few chores around town as punishment and that will be the end of that.'

'The fool. My instructions were to drive people away, not go over and beat Grant to death. I suspected Blocker didn't have the brains of a peanut . . . and he has to go out and prove me right!'

'Martell claims he only told Blocker to throw a scare into Grant and his wife. You know the woman has always been the tough nut of the two.'

Thurmond grit his teeth and pulled a face. 'What insufferable luck. Phoenix Cline!' He waved a hand as if swatting at an invisible insect. 'And he squats in the very spot I'm trying to buy, bargain for, or foreclose on!'

'He also thumped Nape Cod for grabbing hold of Mrs Pomeroy.'

Thurmond's face darkened with ire. 'Nape did what?'

'He had run off a couple of would-be customers at the Pomeroy House and the woman took exception. He claims he was only pinning her arms so she wouldn't hit him. Next thing he knows, he's got a mouthful of dirt and a dent in his skull.'

'The moron!' Thurmond complained. 'First Blocker

kills Grant and now Nape lays hands on a helpless widow! I can't have my men molesting a decent woman – even a hard-headed vixen like Mrs Pomeroy. We'll have the whole town against us.'

'He was too groggy to take on Phoenix alone – didn't know who the guy was at the time – so he went and got Martell.'

'What did Martell do?'

'He got Blocker and they went back to the boarding-house. That's when they learned who the guy was.'

'And the three of them turned tail and ran?'

Race pointed out, 'From the man's reputation, Phoenix Cline is no ordinary man.'

'We need to do some checking and see what that gunman has up his sleeve. Find out where he got the Chinese and what he's planning. He shouldn't be a problem for us if he's just passing through.'

'Martell is going to keep an eye on him,' Race assured him. 'And I was thinking how Amos White's wife is friends with Mrs Baylor. I thought we could have Amos send her to town to do some shopping. With a bunch of Chinese arriving, along with Cline, I'm sure Mrs Baylor will tell her everything that's going on.'

Hildebrand gave a nod of approval. Amos was his cattle foreman, next in line after Race, but he was a simple ranch hand, not a troubleshooter. He worked for the brand, but was about as straight and honest as the summer sun.

'Good thinking. Opal White asking a question or two is not going to cause anyone to get suspicious.'

'You want to do anything about Blocker's hearing?'

'I suppose you ought to be in town and see how the trial goes. If there's a problem, I don't want him saying I instigated his actions. I never once suggested using violence against Grant Pomeroy. However, the man is on the payroll, so I suppose we should offer a degree of support.'

'All right, Boss,' Race said. 'I'll make sure Blocker knows better than to try any finger-pointing over this charge. He'll keep his mouth shut about any orders concerning harassment. Besides, he has a defense – Pomeroy threw the first punch.'

'All right. Get me some answers, Race.'

'You got it, Boss. I'll take care of everything.'

Thurmond watched him leave the house, but his mind was whirling like a leaf sucked up in a dust devil. He had gained control of everything he wanted, except for the Pomeroy House. The widow had been a problem from the very start. It was her tenacity and doggedness which kept the place going. Grant had been weak and would have sold out, but his wife clung to the business like the only shelter in a blizzard. She could not be threatened or reasoned with. Stubborn was simply not a strong enough word for her. The woman was pigheaded beyond all reason. If not for the gravity of the situation, he might have likened her to himself. Her determination was equal to his own, but he wielded might and power, while she had only her pluck. It had been a completely one-sided match, one he would most certainly have won ... except now Phoenix Cline had arrived on the scene.

'Thurmond?' It was his mother. She came into the room and looked around. 'I thought I heard company.'

'It was only Race, Ma. There's some new people in town and he wanted to tell me about it.'

'Race seems an ambitious sort,' she said quietly, though he could tell she didn't approve of him.

'He's handy to have around in case of trouble.'

'I've seen the look in his eyes when you speak about the loading dock. That's something he wants ... even more than you.'

'I know. I shouldn't have promised him he could run it until I had the land. If the Pomeroy House makes a go of it, the loading dock will be a dream turned to dust.'

'Race might think you own him something anyway.'

Thurmond didn't reply to that, watching his mother cross the room. Five feet tall, a mere hundred pounds, wrinkled, with all of her once blond hair turned to gray. He still remembered her as being the beautiful woman who had comforted him during the bad times of his youth. Her feeble steps took her to the divan, where she slumped down, out of breath from the meager exercise. Thurmond moved over and sat down at her side.

'The headaches back?' he asked gently.

'They never seem to go away for long,' she said. 'I hate it when my head gets to hurting so much that I can't knit or read.'

'Maybe we should go to the doctor at Glenwood again.'

She shook her head. 'I always feel worse after seeing him. After the last bleeding treatment I was so tired that I couldn't get out of bed for a week.' She sighed. 'I just get so weary of these headaches and being worn out all the time.'

'I'm sorry, Ma,' he was utterly sincere. 'I wish there some something I could do to make it better.'

She smiled at him. 'You've provided me with my own room in your fine house and a maid to clean and cook for us. You have done much more for me than your father ever did.'

'I've been lucky,' he dismissed her praise.

'I still wish you could find a wife. I feel like I'm holding you back by living here with you.'

'Not a bit, Ma. I'm one of them permanent bachelors. I'll never marry.'

'Well, don't you let my being here stop you from looking. I can't get around very good, but I could be happy in a smaller house, or even an apartment in town.'

He slipped his arm around her shoulders. 'You know how I feel, Ma. You're the only woman in my life.'

'Don't you want children of your own?'

'Naw, I'm too set in my ways to have kids or a woman around trying to change me,' he said. 'I do what I want, when I want, and I like being waited on. Lucinda does everything I need from a woman. . . .' he winked at his mother. 'Well, most everything.'

'So what is happening in town?'

'A gunman with quite a reputation arrived and is staying at the Pomeroy House. He brought a whole bunch of Chinese laborers with him.'

'I read in the newsletter a few weeks ago that the women in Cheyenne, Wyoming, marched in demonstration against some of those people. It had to do with them taking away the laundry business. Do you think that's what they want in Silver Springs, to open a laundry?'

'I don't know, Ma. I sent Race to find out. With Phoenix staying at the Pomeroy place, it could mean the end of my bid for the loading dock and holding pens.'

'You've got enough to keep track of as it is, Thurmond. I don't know how you manage so many businesses all by yourself.'

He smiled at the praise in her voice. His dad had not been a great provider. That's how Thurmond wound up on his own at sixteen. With his every achievement, it seemed his father grew more distant. Perhaps he was jealous of his son's success. When he died, he left his mother with nothing but a pile of debts. The town was going to bury him in a potter's field next to the maintained cemetery, until Thurmond showed up. By the time he finished, his father had a premier site and the largest monument in the entire graveyard.

Nyla lifted a hand and rubbed her brow. Thurmond wished to God he knew how to take away her pain. She suffered in silence for the most part, but he occasionally heard her weeping from the agony. All of his money and he could do nothing for her.

'Why don't you lie down and I'll get you a pan of water and a cloth. It seems to make you feel better when you relax with a damp rag over your forehead and eyes.'

'Thank you, Thurman,' she said, displaying a gracious smile. 'I believe it might help.'

Thurman hurried to get some cool water and a small towel. It helped to be doing something, but he knew it was too little. If only there was something more he could do for her, some way to relieve the damnable pain.

Phoenix had barely taken his boots off when there came a knock at his door. He remained sitting on the bed and said, 'Come on in.'

A man pushed open the door. He was probably in his mid twenties, neatly attired in a dark suit, with polished boots and a city-slicker hat tipped to one side on his head. Entering the room, he removed the hat to reveal a head of thick, although neatly shorn mud-colored hair. His eyes were bright, as if he was a man who enjoyed humor, and a slender smile curled his lips.

'You must be the famous, or should I say infamous, Phoenix Cline.'

'That would be me,' Phoenix replied. 'Who the devil are you?'

He stepped further into the room, closed the door behind him and strode forward with his hand extended. 'Name's William Williams, but I go by Bill.' Another grin, 'My folks didn't have a lot of imagination when it came to names.'

'All right, Bill,' Phoenix allowed, finding the man's grip about right – not weak nor timid, yet he didn't try to demonstrate a superiority with his strength. 'What brings you to my humble abode?'

'I'd like to join in your business venture,' he came right to the point. 'The front office next door used to be mine. My dentist's chair and most of my tools are still there.' He grew serious. 'I can tell you, I wasn't happy when Jim Lyndon foreclosed on my note. I only owed fifty-five dollars and he kicked me out of the building. Shucks, I was barely getting started.'

'From what I've learned, it was likely the influence

of the big dog living outside town rather than the banker himself. The mayor said Hildebrand owns half of the bank and has made it known he wants to develop this part of town.'

'Yes, I'm sure he had a hand in the decision to shut me down.'

'Why would you risk starting your business back up here? The bank might allow you some more credit if you changed locations.'

'I don't like being pushed around,' Bill said.

Phoenix took note of the set to his jaw and determination within his eyes. 'Make your sales pitch.'

'I would need a little money first, enough to pay the note against my chair and tools from the bank. But I assure you, it's a good investment. Anyone can pull a bad tooth, but I can remove the bad and save the good. I use only the latest techniques to drill and utilize a mercury and lead mix to fill teeth so they don't have to be pulled. To save the patient from suffering a lot of pain, I use chloroform to put them to sleep. I graduated from an actual school of dentistry and I'm a fair hand at making false teeth. Big demand for those anywhere there are a lot of people these days.'

'I have a Chinese medico and teacher who is going to use the office, but he might allow you to share the room and do your dentistry. I don't know how much experience he has when it comes to working on people's teeth.'

'I'd pay you a commission out of my fees, providing you can get my tools and chair released. Then, once I've repaid the debt, we could make a fair arrangement concerning the office rent for my future work.'

'You wear a gun like you know how to use one,' Phoenix observed. 'Never heard of an actual dentist who toted a six-iron.'

Bill grinned. 'My dad is a policeman over in Denver. He insisted we boys know how to handle ourselves. My younger brother drives freight and my older brother is a deputy over at Durango, Colorado.'

Phoenix regarded him intently. 'You must know the risk of throwing in with me. It might mean a fight against the most powerful man in the country.'

'I guess I'm a fool for long odds.'

'You wouldn't be sticking your neck out for a pretty face?'

Bill flinched, betraying his feelings, but grinned. 'I presume you don't mean your own. You're talking about Mrs Pomeroy.'

'Men have put their lives on the line for a lot less . . . and she does strike me as something special.'

'Her husband, Grant, never said a decent word to her the whole time I was working in the shop. All that man did was complain and rant about bills and being stuck with her. If Rachel hadn't been his proper wife, I'd have tried to win her away from him.'

'And now?'

'I won't say I'm not interested, but I won't step over the line to court her. I grew up respectful of womenfolk and won't try to rush her into a courtship.'

Phoenix relaxed his peruse. 'You seem an honest and decent man, Bill. You need to speak to Charlie concerning any business arrangement. I don't think there will be a problem, but he's the one in charge of that part of the business.'

'Charlie?'

'The elder statesman of the Chinese. He is setting up his living quarters in the back of your old office. It will serve as a treatment room for his patients as well.'

'He speak English?'

'Better than you and me put together.'

Bill laughed. 'I'll check with him straight away.'

Phoenix told the young man goodbye and he left, closing the door behind him.

Deciding not to simply take his word for everything, Phoenix put on his boots and went down the hallway to the Pomeroy bedroom. He tapped lightly, in case Rachel had gone to bed. There came a rustle of skirts or a robe and the door opened a crack.

'Yes, Mr Cline?' Rachel queried, peeking out through a half-foot opening. Her hair was down about her shoulders, draped like a black satin scarf. She wore a white dressing gown, which she modestly held closed at the throat.

'Sorry to bother you, ma'am,' he apologized. Then he explained about Bill Williams and his offer to open up the dentist office again.

'Mr Williams was always polite and seemed very nice,' she told Phoenix. 'I sure wouldn't wish him any harm. I mean, if there should be trouble. . . .'

'I explained it to him, but he seems ready to accept the risk.'

'Then I ain't got no objection – I'll go along with whatever you decide.'

Phoenix grimaced inwardly at her syntax. He might have smiled about how Charlie would attack the poor unsuspecting lady's grammar, but he remained outwardly serious. 'I wanted to check with you first. After all, you are half owner and should have a say about everything we do.'

Rachel studied him for a moment. He wondered if she had seen his flinch when she'd said, '*ain't got no*'. But it was more than a suspicion he might be poised to make fun of her speech. No, it was like a cat studying a bird on a fence, thinking about whether or not it could spring and catch the bird, or if the effort would be wasted when the bird simply flew away.

'You're a puzzle to me,' she said softly. 'When you stood your ground against the sheriff and his deputies, you had a cold, almost frosty look in your eyes. Yet, when you look at me, you got an odd sort of gleam, kind of like a thirsty man who's being offered a drink of cool water.'

The words stunned Phoenix. Of all the things he might have expected Rachel to say, remarking about his eyes and primitive yearnings. . . . Well, that was downright feminine!

'Uh, I can't say I would ever think of you as a glass of water, Partner. Perhaps a very fine and expensive wine, but not water.'

Rachel giggled at his own analogy. The mirth was candid and spontaneous; it sounded very much like a little girl. It caused Phoenix to laugh too.

'Easy to see why I've never married, huh?' he joked.

Another of those mysterious looks, 'Oh, I don't know,' she said guardedly. 'I reckon comparing someone to an expensive wine could be taken as flattery.'

Phoenix felt suddenly awkward. He reached up to tip his hat in farewell, but he hadn't put on his hat. Feeling an immediate heat rush to his face, he quickly bid Rachel goodnight, spun about and started down the hall. Confused by the first flush of embarrassment he had felt in ten years, he heard her soft reply, 'Goodnight, Mr Cline.'

Charlie had put everyone to work cleaning and preparing to get the laundry and restaurant ready for operation. Bill Williams was there too, working inside the office, setting up his dentist equipment on one side of the room. He would also accept patients for Charlie and make appointments when necessary. Rachel was in the kitchen with Su Lee and Fang Chow, arranging dishes and pots and pans, doing her best to communicate with them. There was much that needed to be done.

Phoenix left them to their labors and was the first customer at the bank when it opened. He entered and met Jim Lyndon, the bank president. A middle-aged man, built on the lean side, he had a narrow face and long neck. His Adam's apple bobbed point-edly against his throat when he spoke, and his suit – faded from wear – was nearly threadbare at the elbows, likely from constant resting on the desktop or teller's counter.

'I've a note of credit from the Denver Bank and Express here,' Phoenix began, offering up the receipt. 'I assume you honor their bank notes.'

Jim took the paper, glanced over it quickly and gave an affirmative nod. 'Yes, I've handled a number of these . . . Mr Cline, is it?'

Phoenix figured the man already knew who he was, but he was being thorough considering Phoenix's name was on the bank draft. He went ahead and introduced himself and extended a hand. After a short . . . rather hesitant shake, he explained his purpose.

'Three things I need from you, Mr Lyndon. First is to open an account with the balance on the Denver bank note. I'll be adding to it or making withdrawals from time to time.'

'That's what a bank is for,' Jim replied. 'And what else?'

'I want to pay off the note against the Pomeroy House, and also the one for Bill Williams, concerning his dental equipment.'

The banker's complexion paled. 'You. . . .' he had to clear his throat. After a moment to compose himself, he added with some reluctance, 'Certainly, I understand.'

Phoenix waited while the man filled out a deposit slip for his voucher, then figured the interest and payoff on the two loans. He subtracted the balances due and gave Phoenix a receipt for the money remaining in his new account.

'Now that you have purchased control of some property in Silver Springs, I presume you are planning to stay in the area,' Jim surmised.

'For a while at least,' Phoenix responded. 'Do you have a newspaper hereabouts?'

'Several doors down the walk. The sign painter and his wife put out a weekly newsletter. You'll see the name on the door – Phil and Irene Douglas.'

Phoenix thanked him and went out the door. He spotted Nape Cod, the deputy he had cold-cocked, loitering across the street. He was about as inconspicuous as someone wearing an Indian war bonnet at a church meeting. The deputy was apparently keeping an eye on him.

Paying him no mind, Phoenix went along the walk until he found the small building with the Douglas name on the front. Inside was a short counter, a desk and a small printing press sitting on one side of the room. A matronly lady looked up from the desk, where she had been busy at work writing something. A professional smile brightened her face.

'Hello there!' she greeted him. 'May I help you?'

Phoenix perused the printing press and smiled. 'My first real job was setting type on a press a bit larger than that one.'

'Really?'

'It was some time back,' he replied, not bothering to tell her how he had been learning the trade, until Lawrence Cline, the editor, was murdered for printing the truth about some powerful crooks who ran the town. When he had taken up a gun and sought justice for the killing, he had been shot three times and died . . . at least, as far as anyone knew. Charlie had mended his wounds and faked his death to prevent further attempts on his life. Phoenix Cline – borrowing the last name of his mentor – had been born. He inhaled and paused to take in the familiar, yet distant, memory.

'It still smells the same, like stepping through a doorway in time and being back at that very newspaper office.'

The lady gave an affirmative nod. 'I know what you

mean. I entered the bakery the other day and it reminded me of my childhood. My mother used to bake fresh bread in the mornings. I had the oddest feeling I was back home.'

Phoenix turned to business. 'I was told you put out a weekly newspaper of sorts.'

'Yes, every Thursday. It's usually only a one page edition, but we sometimes have enough news for two.'

'Do you sell advertising space?'

Her eyes lit up and she rose to her feet. 'Yes, of course. We hardly pay for ink and paper at one cent per newsletter. What did you have in mind?'

'I was thinking about something special.' Then he told her his idea.

The lady could hardly contain her enthusiasm at his proposal. She took down the particulars and promised to have a page to show him by the next morning. Phoenix discussed the price and said he would check back. Rather than turning for the door, he lingered for a long moment, then abruptly spun about and made a hasty exit.

Nape had been standing near the window, trying to see and hear what was going on inside. With Phoenix coming out so suddenly, he was caught eavesdropping. He shuffled his feet, looked down at his shoes and toyed with his belt buckle, pretending he hadn't been watching Phoenix.

'I take exception to being followed, Nape.'

Phoenix's warning caused the man to backpedal, his face showed immediate alarm. 'If you've got a question, you only have to ask.'

'Hold on a minute!' he cried, raising both hands up, palms out, to show he wanted no trouble. 'I don't have no questions.'

Phoenix crowded him back even more. 'No questions, huh? Then you must have something you want to tell me. I mean, why else would you follow me around?'

Nape blubbered: 'No, sir. Uh-uh. I don't want to tell you nothing neither.'

'What about Blocker? Has he been arrested yet?'

Nape tried another step back, but he had inadvertently backed up against the wall of the building. He gulped uncomfortably and would not meet Phoenix's hard stare. 'Well . . . not exactly.'

'What does not exactly mean?'

The sharpness of his tone caused Nape to cower again. 'It's like this, Mr Cline. We . . . um, that is Martell. . . .'

'I'm listening,' Phoenix prompted.

'The trial will be later today,' Nape blurted out. 'Judge Eaton is going to decide the case.'

The news prompted an immediate suspicion. 'Is he going to inform Mrs Pomeroy so she can testify?'

Nape flattened himself against the wall, eyes darting about, as if he was ready to make a break and run for his life, but Phoenix grabbed hold of his shirt

82

and prevented his escape.

'I asked you a question, Nape.'

'The judge said it wouldn't be necessary. He said so long as Blocker was willing to plead guilty, the lady wouldn't have to testify.'

'Guilty? To what charge?'

Nape squirmed in his grasp. 'I don't know. I ain't no lawyer. All I know is Martell said Blocker would say he done it and the judge would sentence him.'

Phoenix let go of the man. 'You best not let me catch you tailing me again, Nape,' he warned. 'I might shoot first, thinking you're a criminal sort, someone trying to back-shoot me. You know what I mean?'

'Yes, sir! I mean, I won't do it no more!' Nape stumbled and almost went to his knees getting turned around. 'I'm going, I'm going!'

As the clumsy deputy hurried away, Phoenix walked over to the general store. It had sounded like a simple plan . . . take Charlie and the other Chinese to a town and set them up. They would open a restaurant and laundry, while Charlie could start his doctoring practice and do a little teaching on the side. A few months of paying him a small portion of their earnings and the debt for the indenture would then be erased. They would be free to work for themselves.

However, he had killed a man to save the Chinese girl. The brother of that man was likely searching for

Phoenix at this very moment, intending to see him dead. Now he had chosen to side a widow, who happened to be perched on the one plot of ground the self-proclaimed king of Silver Springs wanted, but didn't own. Add rescuing the dentist, who had been run out of business to isolate Rachel, and he had done little to ensure peace and tranquility in his life.

Don Baylor was unloading a wagon behind the store, so Phoenix pitched in and gave him a hand. When the chore was done, the two of them sat down on a couple of flour barrels.

'You didn't come here looking for work,' Baylor deduced. 'What new mischief have you been up to?'

'I'm setting up shop over at the Pomeroy House. Anything Charlie – the Chinese man I introduced to you yesterday – or Mrs Pomeroy want, you can charge to me.'

'Sounds like you're staying in a big way.'

'We'll give you a list of things we need each week. You'll probably have to get most of the Chinese restaurant supplies from San Francisco. Will that be a problem?'

Baylor gave his head a negative shake. 'The train ships a lot of stuff from down that way. I can send a telegram to request what I need and it will arrive in a matter of days. I shouldn't have any trouble stocking anything you need.'

'I've an account at the bank, so I can pay you whenever you want.'

'Weekly ought to be fine,' Baylor determined. 'I can pay for each order as we receive it that way.'

Phoenix handed him a piece of paper. 'This is what we need right away and a list of things we'll need for the next order.'

Baylor looked it over. 'I've got most of what you need on hand. Anything I don't have, I'll buy at the pharmacy and pass it along to you at cost. Soon as I finish with that, I'll send off a request to my supplier in San Francisco and get another shipment on the way.'

'Where can I buy some lumber and material for tables and benches?'

'Miller's Construction is at the edge of town. They do most of the building around here and haul directly from a lumber company over near Cimarron. If Miller doesn't have what you need on hand, he can get it right quick.'

'You wouldn't want to take me over to Miller's place and introduce me?'

'I'll do you one better. You tell me what you want and I'll pass it along to him myself. He's a couple weeks late on his bill so I expect your business will help us both out. I'll get him started right away on anything you need.'

Phoenix already had the figures for the lumber and what he wanted done. He handed the paper to Baylor. 'I'm much obliged for your help, Mayor.'

'I'll run this over soon as I send off that order for

supplies.' He glanced over the paper. 'I'm pretty sure Miller has most of this stuff on hand.'

'If he has a couple of carpenters handy, he can send them over too. I'm not sure how handy my Chinese are with a hammer and nails, and I need the work done today.'

'I'll see that you get everything . . . and everyone you need to do the job too.'

'You're a good man, Mayor. I appreciate your help.'

Baylor grinned. 'It's good to be having someone trying to build up a business other than Hildebrand. Since he arrived, he's about taken over Silver Springs.'

'I've yet to meet him, but his name comes up quite often. I wonder, does his influence also cover the judge you have in town?'

'Judge Eaton?'

'Nape told me he is going to preside over Blocker's trial or hearing today. It's already been worked out that he will get off with little more than a scolding.'

Baylor groaned his displeasure. 'That's about as expected.'

'What can you tell me about Eaton? Who appointed him?'

The man chuckled. 'Dag-nab-it! I knew you were going to be more trouble than a sack of wildcats.'

'Yes, well, I've come to learn that true justice often

86

has a high price.'

The mayor put a hard stare on Phoenix. 'I'm wondering if you are willing to pay the price.' As Phoenix's eyebrows elevated in a curious lift, he continued. 'Even for a man like you, it could be an extremely dangerous undertaking to bring real justice to this town.'

'You've got something up your sleeve, Mayor. What is it?'

'There are a lot of unhappy people here, some new arrivals and a few original settlers of Silver Springs. We're all pretty fed up. We've wanted to take a stand against Hildebrand and his methods, but he owns the judge and put his three henchmen in charge of enforcing the law. Other than Blocker beating up Grant, the man hasn't actually broken any laws. It's just that he owns everything in sight and we're taxed to support his thugs.'

'Why do I get the feeling you're going to use the phrase: *but now?*'

Baylor uttered a good-natured laugh. 'Yeah . . . *but now,*' he complied with the prediction, 'now you are here.'

'I'm only one man.'

'Bill Williams once bragged to me about being a fair hand with a gun. The main reason he was driven out of business was because he dared to set up next to Pomeroy's place. And there's also Jody McGuire. He used to handle the chores of town marshal when the occasion called for it. I guess Hildebrand didn't want an honest man that he couldn't control on his payroll, so Jody ended up working at the freight office. And while he's not had a lot of experience, he would be a capable deputy.'

'Deputy?' Phoenix repeated. 'What is an unofficial deputy going to do against Hildebrand and his bunch?'

'If you'll allow me a few minutes of your time, I'll explain how this might work out for all of us.'

Phoenix suffered a knowing dread and lamented, 'This has a really bad sound to it.'

CHAPTER FIVE

Rachel felt the presence of someone and turned to see Bill was standing a few feet from where she was working.

'Expanding the café side, I see,' he said stating the obvious.

'Yes, we've got some planks and wood coming to make more tables and benches. Mr Cline says we can change over to regular tables and chairs, once we are taking in enough money.'

Bill gave his head a nod of approval. 'The man must think the Chinese restaurant will do a lot of business.'

'He said them kinds of eating houses are springing up in a lot of major towns. And Charlie told me there were dozens of them in San Francisco. He says more and more people are eating Chinese-style food.'

'I've been talking to Charlie and he strikes me as about the smartest man I ever met. I was surprised at how much he knew about dentistry.'

'He promised to teach me writing and reading. I know I talk kinda' poorly.'

Bill displayed a smile. 'I like listening to you talk.'

'Yes, but I don't know how to speak like a proper lady. My folks never lived nowhere near a school. All of us kids kinda' had to take care of ourselves.' She lifted her chin. 'I did learn numbers. I'm real good at my pluses and minuses.'

'I'd like to court you proper, soon as you feel ready,' Bill said bluntly.

Rachel was not ready for the statement. She knew Bill had a hankering for her, but to have him come right out and speak of courting. . . .

'I only been widowed for a few weeks, Mr Williams.'

Bill's expression was serious. 'This here country has a real shortage of women, Rachel. You being young and attractive . . . well, that doubles the number of suitors that are going to line up at your door. When you consider you also have a business of your own, there's no end to the number of men who are going to be chasing you.'

Having Bill call her by her first name didn't seem proper, but she let it go. After all, she had known him for several months. Back before he lost his dentist office, he had eaten at the café most every day and been a complete gentleman. Still, the idea of court-ing had not been foremost in her mind, only

struggling to keep the business going. The conclu-
sion barely entered her mind before she had to
admit she had felt something special when Phoenix
was near. He had a way of looking at her that made
her feel pretty and special. His comments had bor-
dered on flattery, yet the words had been harmless,
although warm and sincere. When she met Bill's
hungry stare, she felt uncomfortable. When Phoenix
had locked gazes with her, she felt tingly and alive.

'I ain't ready yet,' she finally told Bill. 'I've too
much to do to be thinking about romance.'

Bill smiled. 'I don't want to put any pressure on
you, Rachel.' He again used her first name. 'But I
wanted to be first on your list of suitors.'

'All right, Mr Williams. I'll let you know if I get to
feeling ready for courting.'

'You could call me by my first name.'

Rachel hesitated, then shook her head. 'We ain't
courting yet. I don't know a lot about he-ing and she-
ing, but I know first names are for more than
acquaintances.'

Bill's smile disappeared. He looked a little uncertain of himself, but quickly recovered. 'Fair enough,
Mrs Pomeroy. I didn't mean to get overly familiar.'

'And I ain't meaning to insult you either,' Rachel
returned without emotion. 'It's just the way it has to
be for now.'

'I understand,' he said. Recovering his aplomb, he
put on a congenial expression. 'If you need anything,

anything at all, you know where to find me.'

Rachel didn't reply to that and watched him walk away. Su came up to her and smiled. 'He like.'

She wondered if it was a question or a statement, but smiled back at the girl. 'Who do you like, Su Lee?' The girl frowned, as if the question was too complicated or she didn't understand the words. 'I guess maybe you need Charlie's permission for courting.'

The girl beamed at the mention of Charlie. 'Uncle Lee good teacher.'

'I'll bet them are the first words he teaches you to say.'

Su knitted her brow, not altogether sure what Rachel meant. She explained it to her a second time and Su laughed. 'Yes, yes,' she continued to laugh. 'Uncle Lee say Uncle Lee vely good teacher.'

'Did I hear you mention my name?' Charlie's voice came from behind them.

Rachel and Su both stopped their laughter and greeted him. Su made a slight bow and then uttered in quite clear English, 'Good morning, Uncle Chong Lee.' Rachel added, 'Hello, Mr Lee.'

'I didn't see you at my first class last night,' Charlie spoke to Rachel.

'I already know how to speak English.'

'Ah, yes, but do you know how to speak it properly?'

Su decided they were going to exchange conversation, so she excused herself and returned to the chore she had been doing before Bill left the room.

'You mean 'cause I don't talk like a proper lady,' Rachel deduced.

'It would take only a small effort on your part. I've also been told you wish to learn to read and write.'

'I kind of thought you would want to work with your own people first,' Rachel said. 'After all, them folks got to learn quick so they can earn a living.'

'Yes, I will teach them as best I can. For you, however, you must learn to read before you can write. And to use proper grammar is the simplest task we can undertake. There are a few rules you can practice for now.'

'What are those rules about?'

'Rules of grammatical construction,' he clarified. 'They are the guidelines which separate those who sound ignorant from those who sound more literate.'

Rachel pulled a face. 'I don't hardly understand what you're talking about.'

'Succinctly put, it is the difference between the language used by a lady as opposed to a street urchin.'

'And, right now, I'm the street person.'

Charlie lifted a finger, pointing to his temple. 'One need only put forth an effort and concentrate to rise above the norm.'

'I'd kinda' like to talk proper educated.'

'The road to success is not a long one, but you

93

must travel it daily.'

Rachel said she would try and Charlie set forth a few rules. Rachel listened intently and vowed to try to remember and put them to use.

Charlie finished the short lecture with, 'We can address some of your other grammatical mistakes when you learn to write. What you see in print will help you to think which words to use when you speak.'

Rachel moved a step closer to Charlie so her words would only reach his ears. 'Could I ask you a personal type question?'

'Certainly, Mrs Pomeroy.'

'How did you become such good friends with Mr Cline?'

Charlie appeared to give the question some thought. Rachel wondered if telling her would betray a confidence with Phoenix. Before she could withdraw her query, Charlie offered his response.

'Baihu suffered several gunshot wounds while performing a community service in a town where I was working. I took him in and we – some of my friends and I – buried an empty coffin at the local cemetery and put his name on the marker. He clearly survived, though, and took a new name, so as to prevent any retribution from some powerful enemies he'd made.'

'You risked your life for him,' Rachel said. 'I see why he thinks so much of you.'

'I had not seen Baihu for several years, until he came to visit a short while back. He had a revelation during his last job and needed my advice.'

'A revelation? Like what's written in the Bible?'

'Not exactly. Anyone can undergo a change of heart . . . which is the kind of revelation I'm speaking of. Baihu wants to make something out of his life, to be more than he was before. It is an admirable goal.'

'Does that have to do with why he is helping me? He ain't. . . .' she caught herself using the taboo word from Charlie's rules. 'I mean he don't even know me.'

Charlie rewarded her effort with a smile and answered, 'Perhaps you have not consulted a mirror recently.' Rachel appeared uncertain of his meaning, but Charlie didn't elaborate. Instead, he returned to his tale concerning Phoenix. 'Baihu has lived for himself since his pretended death. From what he told me about his last job, he learned a valuable lesson and it caused him to seek a new direction in life.'

'What kind of lesson?'

'He discovered that helping oneself is not nearly so gratifying as helping someone else.'

'Is that something that fellow, Confucius, teaches?'

Charlie laughed. 'It is, though his words are much more eloquent.'

'So that's all it is? Mr Cline just happened to choose my place to spend the night, and when he saw I was in trouble, he decided it would be a good deed if he helped?'

'You give yourself too little credit. Did I mention the part about the mirror?'

Rachel tried not to blush, but she felt the fires burn along her cheeks. 'Mr Cline has looked at me some, but I . . . I don't know what he thinks of me.'

'I'm sure he believes you have a good heart. Baihu has a good heart too.'

'Why do you keep calling him *Baihu*?'

'It is the name I gave him.' He shrugged his shoulders. 'He chose to call himself Phoenix, but he will always be a *white tiger* to me.'

Rachel decided they had spoken enough about Phoenix. 'What time is your class tonight?'

'I'll keep Su informed. If you like, the two of you can learn to read and write at the same time.'

'It's real nice of you to help me.'

'Nonsense. You've allowed us to reside with you and start up our business ventures. We are greatly in your debt.'

'Do you really think we're going to get a lot of customers?'

'Baihu is a man of many talents. I think you would do well to stock up on supplies. Not everyone who comes to the restaurant will want to partake of the new cuisine. And we have no menu prepared for breakfast.'

'You're right. I'd better go over and pick up some things at the store.'

Jody McGuire was a good looking young man. Taller than most, he was an inch or two over six feet. After talking to him for a few minutes, Phoenix offered him the job. The fellow immediately took off his work apron and tossed it on a nearby chair.

'Anything beats loading and unloading wagons all day. I've got a mother and sister living at home. I barely earn enough to put food on the table.'

'Thirty dollars a month and two meals a day isn't a lot,' Phoenix cautioned. 'And it could be dangerous as well.'

'I make less than twenty working here and I'm lucky to get ten minutes to eat my own lunch.'

'Well, any fees or fines we take in from lawbreakers are split between us and the judge. That should add a little to your pay each month.'

Jody didn't need convincing. 'I'll pick up my gun and meet you over at the saloon. I imagine that's where this will take place.'

'The trial isn't until this afternoon. I don't expect trouble, but it's best to be prepared.'

Jody snickered. 'Like I said, anything beats what I've been doing the past few months. Plus, I was handling the chores of a city marshal just fine when Martell and his two pets took over. Didn't get so much as a *by your leave* from the bunch of them.'

Phoenix enjoyed his attitude. He had immediately

liked the young man. He was physically fit from the hard work he did and claimed to be a fair shot with either a pistol or long gun. Plus, he had the respect of the original settlers, having proven he could carry a badge, before Hildebrand appointed his own lawmen. When he considered the chore ahead, he realized he would need a deputy he could depend on.

He left the freight company office and Jody hurried off to tell his boss he was quitting. Jody would be at the Palace Saloon before the trial started and Bill had promised to be there as well. Add the mayor and a couple businessmen Don promised would stand up with him and it gave him the support he would need.

Phoenix took a quick survey about town, but there was nothing suspicious going on. Of course, there was no reason yet. He hadn't made his first big move. After that. . . ?

Thurmond listened to the report from Race. Amos' wife had spoken to Mrs Baylor and passed along the information. Amos had then told Race all she had learned.

'You say the Chinese are indentured?' he clarified with his ramrod.

'Yep. I sent a cable to San Francisco. That's where Phoenix picked up the Chinese. The telegrapher replied that Phoenix was in a gunfight and killed the man who held the indenture, along with another man, and wounded two others. He didn't know much else, other than Phoenix paid the balance of the indenture so the Chinese were his. As for the killings, no charges were brought against him.'

'He shot four men – killed two of them – and there were no charges at all? How could he get away with something like that?' Thurmond wanted to know.

Race made a helpless gesture. 'Got me.'

Thurmond was impressed. 'By gadfry! I wish the man was working for me. Anyone who can pull off something like that. . . .'

'He must be quite a story teller,' Race replied to the open-ended sentence.

'I'll say,' Thurmond agreed. 'The man's not only hell on the hoof with a gun, he must also have some wits about him.'

Race changed subjects. 'As I was leaving town, I seen a load of lumber headed toward the Pomeroy House. Amos's wife said Mrs Baylor was tickled to have Phoenix and the coolies in town. Guess he has placed orders for a couple hundred dollars worth of supplies already. The man seems to be taking over everything around the Pomeroy House.'

'Looks as if I can say goodbye to the idea that Baylor will be forced to sell out to me. I had hoped to own his store before winter.'

'And Phoenix throwing in with Mrs Pomeroy is going to make it that much harder to get her to sell.'

'What did Jim Lyndon have to say?'

'Phoenix paid off the debts against both the Pomeroy House and the dentist.'

'The dentist too? What's he doing paying off his bill?'

'The Chinese are going to open a laundry and restaurant. As for Williams, I'm guessing he is going to reopen his dentist office. Also, Amos's wife said one of those squinty-eyed coolies is a doctor too.' Race set his teeth to restrain his anger. 'That guy butting into our affairs is going to ruin everything!'

'It does seem as if Phoenix has turned the tables on us.'

Race swore vehemently. 'A blasted, high-handed gunman rides in and decides he wants to set up shop for his Chinese pals, and we stand to lose out on ever building our loading dock!'

Thurmond paid no attention to his employee's frustration. 'You say one of the new arrivals is a doctor?'

'One of the Chinese, so Amos's wife said.'

Thurmond set aside his wonder about a far-eastern doctor of medicine and expelled a long breath, a resignation of defeat. 'I'm afraid Phoenix has trumped our ace. We've lost our leverage against Mrs Pomeroy. It sounds as if her boarding-house will soon be supported by a laundry, a bigger restaurant and a medical office. Plus, Baylor's store has a new customer paying him money by the fistfuls. Phoenix has come into our lives like a pox, a blight which has spread throughout that entire side of town.'

'I was counting on that there big promotion, boss,' Race said bitterly. 'I don't like the idea of letting one man destroy everything we had planned.'

'We won't wave the white flag just yet. Let's give this a little time and see how it plays out.'

Race grit his teeth, seething with anger. 'It's a good thing we've got the law sewed up tight or Phoenix would ruin that for us too.'

Pacing the floor, Thurmond considered riding in to town for Blocker Quade's hearing. If something went wrong, he would be there to take action. He dismissed the idea at once. He didn't feel like making the ride. It was windy and the dusty road was deeply rutted from the last rain. Besides, Race would be there, along with his other appointed lawmen. What could possibly go wrong?

'What time is the trial?' he asked Race.

'In less than an hour. I've got to get going, but Judge Eaton knows better than to cross us. I don't think we have anything to worry about on that front.'

'I'm sure you're right.' Thurmond was thinking hard. 'All the same, you best get to town and see if Phoenix has made any other changes. If he decides to run for governor or something, I want to know about it.'

Race displayed a blank expression.

'I'm kidding,' Thurmond informed him.

'Oh, yeah, right! Good one, Boss.'

Race left the room and, for a long moment, Thurmond stared off into space. He remembered back to when he had left home. Striking out on his own, while not yet seventeen, he had worked several years at diggings and around mines for his keep. He'd struck gold when a crippled miner had taken him in and made him a partner. The good-hearted man died a year later from consumption. Thurmond sold the mine and bought his first gambling house – a one room shack in a mining camp. He started with nothing but a couple of tables, some chairs and several bottles of whiskey. After a short while, he was able to buy a roulette table and wheel. He spent two hard years in that rundown shanty, before he moved on and opened a bigger casino. Several years later, he owned a major saloon and casino, with a stage on which dancing girls, theater groups or entertainers could perform. Every step had lifted him higher, until he had moved to Silver Springs and practically bought the town.

As for his folks, he had written them a few times over the years – his mother always replied and wished him everything in the world. The one time he had visited home, his old man hadn't seemed happy to see him. Now he was gone and his mother was here living on his ranch. Everything had settled into place . . . other than for the Pomeroy House. Phoenix Cline had come into his life and prevented further growth.

With the idea of adding loading docks, he had promised Race his own enterprise. He knew his ramrod was unhappy at the change of fortune and might cause trouble. He might even try to have Phoenix killed. That was unacceptable.

Thurmond had done a great many things that were questionable, but he had never crossed the line to criminal activity. Oh, there were those who considered extortion, pressure, and a bit of arm twisting as unethical, but it was no different from being a politician. He allowed himself a grim smile. Well, unlike a politician, he couldn't be voted out of office.

His reverie was interrupted by Nyla Hildebrand. She entered the room carrying a tray with coffee and cookies in her trembling hands. He hurried to take it from her and set on the tea table.

'Ah-h-h,' he inhaled deeply. 'Freshly baked cookies.'

'Your favorites,' she replied happily. 'I had to arm wrestle Lucinda, but I made the cookies myself.'

'You shouldn't be working over a hot stove.'

'I remember how you always loved sugar cookies when you were growing up.'

'Yes,' he said, picking one up and taking a big bite. 'Umm, as good as ever. I can't believe you remember how to bake something after nearly thirty years.'

'I made them for your father once in a while. He never liked them as much as you, but he always ate them all within a few days.'

103

'You must miss him terribly.'

She poured a cup of coffee, added a bit of cow's milk and some sugar, then began to stir it about with a spoon. When she spoke, it was as if she was speaking to herself.

'Leo wasn't an easy man to love. He didn't like anyone who did anything better than he did himself. That's why he had a hard time working for someone else. He was always thinking he could do the job better.'

'I know I never did anything to please him, no matter how hard I tried.'

'He was a demanding man,' she maintained. 'I was often glad you were our only child. I don't know how he would have handled any more kids. He drove you away before you even had a chance to become a man.'

'He didn't earn enough to feed the three of us,' Thurmond said. 'It was either find work or starve, and there were no jobs close by to be had. I had to go to the mine fields to find work.'

'You're a good boy, Thurmond. I'm very proud of you.'

The bite of cookie lodged halfway down his throat. Thurmond coughed noisily. Until Nyla had come to live with him, he had thought of no one else in the world but himself. He had conned, pressured and cheated people and generally done whatever it took to get what he wanted. Hardly something a mother would be proud of.

Thurmond, although powerful and dogmatic, was nonetheless honest in his evaluation of himself. Average looking at best, with a slight paunch hanging over his belt, just under five-and-a-half-foot tall, with a receding hairline and a self-serving disposition. He knew the value of a dollar and enjoyed the feeling of power and control which came with having money. He cared little for social functions and had never been serious about a woman. He didn't want a nag hanging around, second guessing his decisions or trying to influence him. Neither did he want a dependent, completely submissive female, one who was content to be his doormat. Even a gal somewhere in between didn't seem all that desirable. To his way of thinking, Lucinda did most chores he needed a woman for . . . and anything else he needed only cost a few dollars anytime he wanted it. As for kids, he didn't crave that kind of misery. If he wanted someone around to keep him company, he'd get a dog.

CHAPTER SIX

It was a small crowd at the saloon. A desk and chair for the judge had been placed up on the stage, while the chairs from the gambling tables had been set up for the spectators. It was more a performance for paying customers than an actual court proceeding. Martell, Nape and a couple of men Phoenix didn't know were seated near Blocker. Those mustered on the opposite side were the mayor, Mr and Mrs Douglas from the newspaper and another two or three who were from out of town. A handful of curious onlookers filled up the rest of the seats. Jody had stationed himself on one side of the room, while Bill was on the other. Both wore guns and gave Phoenix a nod to show they were ready.

Judge Eaton took his place behind the desk, cleared his throat and called for silence. Then he peered around the room through hung-over, red-rimmed eyes and made a formal announcement.

'This here court is now is session. We're here today so I can judge the case of Blocker Quade, in the matter of the death of Grant Pomeroy.' He paused to look over at Blocker. 'You are a deputy sheriff for our fair town and this happened while you were on duty. Do you have an explanation concerning this event?'

The big man rose to his feet. 'Grant come at me and threw the first punch; he started the fight,' Blocker avowed. 'But I admit I hit him a couple times after he was down. I guess I must have hit him too hard.'

'Sounds as if you were defending yourself, but are guilty of using a measure of excessive force,' Eaton commented.

'Reckon that's about the whole story, Your Honor.'

'I've been informed you are willing to plead guilty to the charge of Unintentional Manslaughter. Is that true?'

'Yes, sir.'

'Then I so rule and declare you should spend thirty days doing chores around town to complete your debt to—'

'If you'll pardon the interruption, Judge,' Phoenix stopped his verdict. He moved forward to stand at the base of the stage. 'I am here to challenge the court in this matter.'

Eaton scowled down at Phoenix. 'Who do you think you are, sonny! You can't speak up in my court unless I give you permission!'

'There's a clear conflict of interest concerning this trial,' Phoenix stated professionally, ignoring the man's ire. 'I respectfully request that you recuse yourself from this case.'

Eaton opened his mouth to protest, then frowned. 'Recuse? What in thunderation does that mean?'

'It means you should withdraw from the case. Both you and Blocker work for the same man.'

'I've never heard of such nonsense. I'm the judge here in Silver Springs and I say what can and can't go on in a court of law!'

Phoenix held his ground. 'You should think about what I'm saying, Judge. If you want to carry this forward, you will regret it.'

'No one threatens me in my own courtroom!' Eaton bellowed. 'I'll have you thrown in jail for contempt of court!'

Phoenix shook his head. 'I'm sorry, but you have no authority to do that, Mr Eaton,' he said, purposely eliminating his formal title. 'The truth is, you have no judicial power in the state of Colorado.'

Eaton blanched at this statement, a stark expression contorting his face. He sat with his mouth open, unable to reply to the statement.

Phoenix rotated to address those in the courtroom, rather than continuing to face the judge. 'I've done some checking on Mr Eaton's background,' he began. 'He was a jack-leg lawyer over in Green River, Wyoming, and was appointed judge by the town mayor. However, his position was rescinded when a new mayor was elected a couple years back. In the eyes of both Federal and State law, he has no standing in Silver Springs other than as a spectator.'

'Sheriff Martell!' Judge Eaton squeaked hoarsely. 'Arrest this man for disrupting my court!'

Phoenix pinned Martell and Nape with a warning gaze, stopping them both cold. Neither man chose to rise or intervene, fearful Phoenix would kill them on the spot.

'If I might have the floor,' Don Baylor spoke up, rising to his feet. 'I believe I can clear up this confusion.'

Eaton's color returned, his fury contained, and he glowered at the mayor. 'Confusion!' Eaton snapped. 'We've no confusion, only an open contempt for this court and the judicial system!'

Baylor waved a hand to dismiss Eaton's ranting and held the floor.

'As mayor of Silver Springs, it is my responsibility to appoint a sheriff, until or unless one is elected through nomination or voting. I never officially endorsed Martell or his deputies. They assumed authority through intimidation, but none of them have any official standings in Silver Springs.'

'What are you talking about, Don?' Eaton cried out. 'Martell is the sheriff and I'm the judge! It's been that way since the railroad arrived.'

'I remember when you and Martell took over,

Fred.' Baylor called the judge by his first name. 'But you were never a real judge, and Martell, Nape and Blocker are only hired hands, all working for Mr Hildebrand. He's a businessman without the authority to appoint anyone to the position of judge or sheriff.'

Eaton was blubbering inanely, trying to make sense of what was happening. He rose up from his desk and waggled a finger at Phoenix.

'This is all your doing!' he wailed. 'You've ruined everything, you dirty, low-down, worthless. . . .'

'Better watch what you say, Fred,' Baylor shut him down. 'I've appointed Phoenix Cline sheriff of Silver Springs.' He grinned at the man's shocked expression, as the news sank in. 'I'd hate to see you locked up for insulting an officer of the law.'

Those words brought a round of laughter and snickers from the audience.

Phoenix fixed his attention on Martell and Nape. 'You two can turn in your badges when you return Blocker to his cell. We're going to have a circuit judge come to oversee the trial for Blocker. The charge is Manslaughter.'

The big man swore and shook his fist at Phoenix. 'I told how it happened. Grant attacked me! He threw the first punch!'

'Yes, after you began to molest his wife forcibly. I'm sure the judge will take all of the facts into account.'

Blocker spun on Martell for help, but the ex-sheriff saw Bill had come forward to stand alongside Phoenix. When he looked the other direction, Jody was standing with his gun trained on the three of them.

'What do you think you are you doing. McGuire?' Martell asked Jody.

'I'm Phoenix Cline's deputy,' he answered. 'I thought I would tag along with you boys . . . just to make sure the three of you don't get lost on your way to the jail.'

Race Killroke got up from his chair and stormed out of the room. The others began to file out too. Jody and Bill both went with Martell, Nape and Blocker to the jail.

'You're welcome to stay in town, Fred,' Baylor explained to the deposed judge, 'but the free ride is over. I doubt Hildebrand will want to pay you for doing nothing, and the city of Silver Springs will be appointing a new, impartial judge.'

Eaton displayed a hang-dog look. 'Don, how can you do this to me?'

'Phoenix gave you a chance to recuse yourself. You didn't take it.'

'Take it?' he cried. 'I didn't even know what the word meant!'

'Sorry, Fred, but that's the way it is. We're going to have law and order in Silver Springs, and it's going to be for all of the people equally.'

111

'Any last words for the newspaper?' Phil Douglas asked Fred Eaton.

'Yes!' he snapped. 'But you won't dare print them, not unless you want the new sheriff to throw you in jail!'

Baylor and his friends came over and congratulated Phoenix. The mayor smiled and said, 'Guess I'll have to get around to appointing a new judge.'

'Good idea. We might be needing one real soon.'

Baylor looked around at the other businessmen. 'Any volunteers?'

Phoenix left the men discussing plans for the city and walked along with Mr and Mrs Douglas to their office. The lady had indicated she had the layout for his advertising ready. They all gathered around the editor's desk and he looked the page over.

When Phoenix had worked with Lawrence Cline, it had been on a much bigger scale, but the printing and wording had turned out very nice. He scanned it for accuracy and gave his approval.

'When can this edition be ready?'

'Tomorrow, if you want,' Douglas said. 'We need to add the announcement about your taking over as sheriff and the judge being de-robed.'

Phoenix chuckled. 'Are you sure de-robed is the right word?'

'Probably dethroned would work,' Irene spoke up. 'De-robed sounds rather risqué.'

They all laughed, and then Phoenix paid for the

112

advertising, plus an extra dollar so they could give away a hundred copies. Then he headed for the jail.

Charlie helped to line out everyone's job. With Bill to watch the doctor/dentist office, he was able to get the laundry organized. Bo Wang, who had learned to speak a little more English than the others in that group, would be the one to accept orders and run the makeshift counter. As soon as business warranted, they would add some cubicles for storing finished laundry orders. For a cash drawer he had a cigar box.

In the restaurant, Su Lee was to help Rachel take orders and wait on customers, while Guang Sung was in charge of the cooks and table clearing crew. The supplies they had picked up at Baylor's store were enough to get them by until the order arrived from San Francisco.

Rachel oversaw Miller's workers as they fashioned the new tables and benches. Charlie came in and paused to watch, so Rachel moved over to stand next to him.

'We've got room for lots of customers now,' Rachel said, as they watched the construction going on around them. 'Mr Cline said we ought to be able to feed thirty or more at one time.' She showed a puzzled mien. 'I don't know how he intends to get so many people to come here to eat.'

'Baihu is a man of many facets.'

'Do that mean something good . . . facets?'

Charlie smiled at her lack of understanding. 'He stood and fought against four men to save Su Lee from being placed in a Joy House. Next, he managed to get all the others released in his care. He did this without putting himself on the outs with the law. I can't think of anyone else who could have done that.' Charlie grunted his admiration. 'He is singular to any man I have ever known or read about. He is an enigma, Mrs Pomeroy.'

'I don't know what that there enigma is, but he does have a way of getting things done. Where did he find all these men to build the tables and benches?'

'Some are from the lumber company and several are men from around town whom the mayor asked to help.'

Rachel was again perplexed. 'I don't understand anything that's happened. He went to see that Blocker didn't get away with killing Grant, and he returns as the town sheriff!'

'Remember my words of a moment ago? Baihu is more than an ordinary man.'

'You said he saved Su Lee from some kind of house?'

'A Joy House. It is a place where men can spend a few dollars and sample the favors of a young lady. There are many in the Chinese districts throughout California.'

'That sweet young girl!' Rachel was appalled.

'Someone was going to put her in one of them sin-to-Moses places?'

'Yes, but, as I mentioned, Baihu prevented it.'

Rachel folded her arms as if overwhelmed. 'He done that. Then he comes here and saves me from being pawed at by Nape and run out of business. Next thing, he's wearing the badge as the new sheriff. Goodness, Charlie, is Phoenix trying to save the whole world?'

'It is who he has become. He started out trying to make his own way, but now he wants to make a difference. I applaud his altruistic ambition, although it might mean his death. There are many enemies to be made when trying to restore a measure of justice within a corrupted community.'

'I don't want to see him get hurt,' Rachel said. 'He's the first man I ever.. . . .'

When she didn't finish, Charlie cast a look of wonder at her. He observed Bill had come into the room and had moved within earshot.

'I've a customer who needs a doctor,' he spoke to Charlie. 'One of the farmer women broke her finger.' He grimaced. 'She thinks you might have to cut it off.'

'We shall see if I can save the finger. Excuse me,' he bid goodbye to Rachel and hurried to attend to the woman. Bill hesitated for a moment and smiled.

'Looks like we're in business. The farmer lady was looking for Vaughn and Mrs Baylor told her about

Charlie.' When Rachel didn't respond to that, he looked at all the work being done. 'You must be expecting a passel of hungry people tomorrow.'

'Mr Cline said we should be ready for a full restaurant.'

'The man is an optimist, I'll give him that.'

'Yes,' she agreed, uncertain as to what an optimist was. 'He is a very special kind of man.'

Before he could mask it, a flash of jealousy washed over Bill's face. He added with a degree of reluctance. 'One of a kind.'

'An enigma – that's what Charlie called him,' Rachel avowed.

Bill laughed out loud at her choice of words. 'I'll go along with Charlie.'

'Mr Cline saved Su Lee from being forced to serve in a Joy House. That's a Chinese pay-for-favor type place.'

The information sobered Bill. 'No kidding?' He clicked his tongue. 'Makes me wish I was a writer. I'll bet a man could make some real money selling stories about the exploits of Phoenix Cline.'

'I only hope he don't get himself killed.'

'The man rides a dangerous trail, Mrs Pomeroy. You might want to think twice about setting your cap for him.'

The remark caused her an instant annoyance. 'I'll thank you to keep your opinions to yourself, Mr Williams. I don't need you to advise me about who I

116

should like or dislike.'

'I'm sorry,' Bill backpedaled from his comment. 'I just thought I should point out how someone who takes chances like Phoenix Cline might get himself killed.'

'It takes a brave man to oppose four men to save a young girl from a life of shame, or stand up against a man as powerful as Thurmond Hildebrand and his band of ruffians.'

'I would be the first to agree.'

'And don't you be thinking I'm the sort to give my affections to a man just because he comes to my defense.'

'No, I'm certain you're not,' Bill agreed again, shaking his head vigorously.

'You got no idea as to what I'm feeling.' Rachel might have finished with *because I don't know what I'm feeling myself*!

'Yes, ma'am,' Bill murmured weakly, completely cowed by her outburst.

Flustered, with no outlet other than to make poor Bill feel worse, Rachel said a quick goodbye and went to see how Su Lee was doing. It vexed her that she had exploded for no reason. She knew Bill had only been trying to warn her of the danger of falling for a man like Phoenix. But the intense feelings inside Rachel seemed to be at war. She had no control over them. What had caused that to happen? Surely this kind of reaction wasn't love. Love was supposed to be dreamy, exciting and wonderful. This was a night-mare of uncontrollable emotions.

CHAPTER SEVEN

Phoenix arrived at the big ranch house and reined up at the hitching post out front. He had dismounted when a mildly paunchy, though still imposing, man opened the door.

'You would be Phoenix Cline,' was his greeting.

'Mr Hildebrand, I presume.'

There was no animosity in the man's face, only a measure of curiosity. He said, 'Yes. What can I do for you?'

'I wanted you to have a copy of tomorrow's paper,' Phoenix said, offering him the page Mrs Douglas had printed off.

The man scanned the advertisement and laughed with amusement. 'I have to hand it to you, Cline, you wasted no time getting settled. Here two days and you wind up sheriff and have three different businesses going. Until you arrived, I used to think I was ambitious.'

'I kind of got tagged with a bunch of indentured workers,' Phoenix explained. 'I needed to find a place for them.'

'We could use a good, inexpensive laundry in town,' Hildebrand said. 'As for the dentist, I hated to see him forced out of business. Of course,' he didn't hide the truth, 'I did need him to vacate his office, so I could encourage the Pomeroys to sell. Looks like I can forget about that piece of land altogether now.'

'Mrs Pomeroy strikes me as having a bit of a stubborn streak. I'm not sure she would have ever sold the place.'

'No, I'm sure you're right.'

'You don't seem all that upset,' Phoenix said candidly. 'I came here expecting to get a warning, maybe even a death threat.'

Hildebrand harrumphed dismissively. 'I earned my way by taking gambles, Mr Cline. I've won my share and lost a few as well. It taught me one of life's important lessons – no matter how good you are at something, you aren't going to win every time.'

'My friend, Charlie, would probably quote something from Confucius for you that would mean about the same thing.'

'Charlie . . . the doctor listed here in your advertisement?'

'Yes, he's a very knowledgeable sort.'

'How about his medical skills?'

'In my opinion, he's far ahead of most quacks you

meet west of Denver. Of course, the man saved my life, so I'm bound to be a little biased.'

'I wonder if he would come out here and examine my mother?'

'Your mother?'

'She suffers severe headaches and is quite rundown. I don't expect her to hop around like a spring chicken, as she is almost sixty years old, but she often can't sleep or even do modest chores from the constant pain.'

'Soon as I get back to town, I'll have him ride out here. That is,' he corrected, 'I'll hitch up the buggy for him. Charlie doesn't ride horses.'

'That's very good of you, Mr Cline.'

'So, there're no hard feelings over the Pomeroy House?'

Hildebrand uttered a sigh of resignation. 'I'm disappointed, but I learned a long time ago that holding a grudge was a waste of effort. This is one of the times I didn't win,' he concluded. 'I can live with it.'

'I'm glad you took the high road about this.'

'Not at all,' he said. 'And I want Mrs Pomeroy to know, I never gave the order for anyone to harm either her or Grant.' He grimaced as if he felt a pang. 'I admit I advised Martell that I wanted to buy their place, but no one was to get hurt. I have never resorted to violence to get what I wanted.'

'I suppose your mother wouldn't like it?' Phoenix teased.

Hildebrand laughed out loud. 'Yes, something like that. Can't have her being ashamed of her only child.'

'Charlie ought to be here in an hour or so. I hope he can do something for her.'

'Thank you, Mr Cline. I wish you success here in Silver Springs.'

Phoenix mounted his horse, gave a nod of his head, and rode out of the yard. Of all the scenarios he had run through in his mind, the meeting with Hildebrand was completely unexpected!

That evening, Phoenix was summoned by Jody when a fight broke out between several cowboys from two rival spreads. It ended the moment he entered the room and all six of those involved paid damages to the saloon. Then Don Baylor was forced into the role of judge and issued a fine of five dollars each. He put his half of the fees in the city coffers, while Jody and Phoenix split the other half. It had been their first successful night as sheriff and deputy, but Phoenix ended up losing most of his night's sleep.

It felt as if he had barely dozed off when someone knocked at the door to his room. Phoenix groaned, blinking at the early-morning light and said 'just-a-minute'. He pulled on his pants and then opened the door to find Rachel standing there with a wild, almost panicked look on her face.

'What is it, Mrs Pomeroy?'

'Did . . . did you do this?' she gasped, shoving a large sheet of paper at him.

Phoenix recognized the newsletter at once. 'Yes, I was going to talk to you about it, but kind of lost track of time yesterday.'

'B-but. . . .' She sputtered. 'Charlie read it to me! He said this paper says we're offering free meals!'

'Only one free meal with each newspaper. The customer will give you the paper and they get a free meal.'

She appeared flabbergasted. 'But . . . but how can we do that? I mean, we'll go broke giving food away for free!'

'Not at all,' Phoenix assured her. 'We have to get people down here to try the Chinese food. Many folks around here have never tasted chow mein or wontons or fried rice. Besides, there're only a hundred copies being printed up, so most of them will be gone after the first day or two.'

Rachel still had a lost look on her face. 'What else does it say?' she asked. 'I only asked Charlie when I seen the word "Free", cause I know that word.'

Phoenix held the paper and pointed as he spoke. 'This is about the laundry and our rates – first item is free when you drop off at least three garments. And here's the part about Bill and Charlie, saying how Bill is an accredited dentist and Charlie is a qualified doctor and pharmacist. Both offer painless procedures because they use chloroform to put the patient

123

to sleep.' He allowed the information to sink in for a few seconds. 'Do you understand why I did this?'

The woman's eyes were glazed, as if she was in a trance. 'Uh-huh,' she muttered. 'I've got a partner who's plum crazy.'

Charlie appeared in the hallway. He hesitated until he could see he wasn't interrupting and came forward.

'I hope we have enough food on hand for so many customers. When you told me to purchase supplies to serve a large number of people, I thought you intended it to mean perhaps thirty or forty.'

'Don Baylor has an order on the way,' Phoenix informed him, and then asked, 'Laundry all ready for operation?'

'Yes, we have the washing tubs filled, the drying lines are in place, and three irons and tables are set up for pressing clothes.'

'And you and Bill?'

'We are prepared for business as well. I was able to save a broken finger for one of the local farmer ladies yesterday. I believe that will garner some customers.'

'How about Mrs Hildebrand? Were you able to help her?'

Charlie gave his head a bob. 'She suffers from migraine headaches. The doctor she had been seeing was compounding her problem through use of the archaic remedy of bleeding. Such barbaric and outdated treatment caused more fatigue and made the poor lady even more susceptible to the headaches.'

'I suppose you gave her some of your all-purpose ginseng tonic?'

'To be used when she first feels a headache coming on,' Charlie confirmed. 'There is little other treatment that offers relief for migraines.'

'You done went out to the Hildebrand place?' Rachel was astounded. 'Both of you have been out there . . . and neither of you are dead?'

'The man was most pleasant and appreciative,' Charlie said.

'Now we'll see if this plan of mine to bring in business works,' Phoenix said, getting back to the present. 'Mrs Pomeroy was just expressing her enthusiasm for the idea. She will accept one newspaper as payment for a single meal.'

'We should have an abundance of newsletters by the end of the day,' Charlie quipped. 'We can use them to stoke the fires for heating water for the laundry.' He grinned. 'That way, you will get something in return for the money you've spent.'

'Advertising is the best way to get people down here to try the food. Once they try it, a good many of them will come back again.'

'Confucius says, *The cautious seldom err*,' he quoted. 'I imagine you have made many mistakes, Baihu.' Then with a smile, 'But those who do not try, succeed only at being stagnant or lazy.'

Phoenix laughed as Charlie did an about-face and started back down the hallway. He watched him for a moment and then looked back at Rachel. She had an odd sort of upward lift to her lips, as if she found something amusing, but was trying hard to not laugh or smile.

'What?' he asked, perplexed by the mysterious expression.

'You and Charlie seem like a father and son.'

'I was orphaned at six years old, so I don't remember a lot about my father. I was fortunate that a newspaper man took me in for several years. He was the only father I remember. As for Charlie, he is all about communication and integrity.'

'He's a good teacher too, though he's pretty strict. He expects a lot from his students.'

'You got all of that out of one class?'

'Not just at class. He's give me other stuff to learn. I'm doing my letters and he thinks he can learn me to read in a short amount of time.'

'I'm sure he would tell you that he can teach you, but you must do the *learning*.'

'I said it wrong, didn't I?'

Phoenix put encouragement into his voice. 'You'll pick it up once you start reading. Besides, there are a great number of people around who can't read.'

'Mr Williams wants to court me.'

Rachel made the statement out of thin air. It took

a moment before it penetrated Phoenix's skull. He couldn't prevent the instant frown which drew his brows closer and prompted a tightness of his jaw. Worse, a knot twisted within his chest, as if someone had suddenly grabbed him in a bear hug and was trying to crush the air from his lungs.

When Phoenix didn't speak, Rachel said, 'I told him it was too soon.' She waited a moment and spouted, 'Ain't . . . I mean, isn't it?'

Phoenix cast a yearning look down the hallway, wishing Charlie were there to answer her question. 'Uh, well, I suppose it depends on how much you loved your husband.'

'Weren't never no question of love between us,' Rachel was candid. 'He didn't want me and I was sold to him to make things better for my folks. We got along most of the time, but he never wanted me.'

'Sounds like a poor arrangement for you both,' Phoenix sympathized.

'So how long do you think is proper to wait until I should accept an offer of courting?'

'I don't really know, Mrs Pomeroy,' he replied. Then, hating each word that followed: 'Do you want to take Bill up on his offer?'

Rachel had been regarding him with a wide-eyed innocence. Oddly, his question caused her to lower her gaze, as if trying to hide her immediate response.

'Bill is a nice man and gentlemanly too,' she murmured. 'But I don't got any special feelings for him.'

'Well, with so many men and so few women in this part of the country, you'll get plenty of offers. It's probably just as well to keep your options open.'

Rachel shifted her feet nervously and asked softly, 'What about you?'

'Me?'

'You kind of flirted with me before. Was that real, or was you just making fun with me?'

Now it was Phoenix who felt ill-at-ease. 'I wouldn't make fun of you, Mrs Pomeroy. I think you're about as precious as the first spring rain.'

The statement caused her head to lift. 'Precious,' she repeated the word. 'Is that like saying you would want to court me too?'

This whole situation was about as uncomfortable as discovering ants in your trousers at a church picnic. Did a man shout and holler for help, drop his drawers and start swatting, or simply make a mad dash for the hills? He found Rachel enticing, beautiful and charming. She had grit, determination and strength. Phoenix knew it took a lot of courage for her to speak to him in such a way. She had been bartered like a horse, forced into a marriage to a man she didn't even know. That had to have squashed her self-worth and confidence. Yet, she was standing an arm's length away, risking total humiliation and embarrassment, boldly asking a man if he wished to court her.

'Rachel,' Phoenix whispered her first name. 'I'm

not worthy of someone as fine as you. I've killed several men in gunfights. I've sold my gun to the highest bidder, not always knowing if I was even on the right side. I'd be the proudest man on earth to have you on my arm, but you deserve a much better suitor than me.'

The young woman didn't reply, but stepped forward and slipped her arms around Phoenix. He hesitated only a moment before he encircled her within his embrace. Rachel leaned against him, resting her head against his chest and hugging him tightly. After a few seconds, she stepped back, whirled about and hurried down the passageway. Phoenix was left standing there, his brain on fire, his heart pounding, lost in a bewilderment of awe and euphoria.

Martell waved to Nape and the two met in the alley a short way from the jail. Moving a few steps so they would not be seen, Martell grunted his disgust.

'So much for Race's idea of starting a fight between the Slash T and some of our riders last night,' he complained. 'Who'd have thought that blasted dentist would show up!'

Nape agreed. 'Yeah, drawing the deputy over to the fracas, I figured we could get Blocker out with no trouble. Instead, Bill arrives to watch the jail and Phoenix goes over with Jody and puts an end to the fight. Who's going to mess with him?'

'We'll have to try it some other way.'

'Yeah, but Race warned that we shouldn't hurt Jody, cause he's so popular around town.'

'I've an idea that will work, and we won't have to worry about Jody. Phoenix will be watching the jail tonight. I heard the two of them are going to trade off nights while they have a prisoncr.'

Nape scratched his head. 'That don't sound any easier for you and me. I'd rather take my chances with Jody.'

'I've got a simple but workable plan, Nape. Blocker will have to leave the country, but this is our best chance to go back to the way it was before.'

'That only works if Phoenix Cline ends up dead.'

Martell snorted. 'Trust me, that's a big part of this plan. And it'll get us an extra hundred dollars from Race.'

'I miss being paid for wearing a badge, and that's the truth,' Nape said. 'Tell me how we are going to handle Phoenix Cline.'

Hectic was the best word to describe the beginning of the day for the Pomeroy House and its two new enterprises. By the time they opened the door, Charlie had a dozen customers lined up and Bill had three. Word had gotten around how Charlie had treated Mrs Hildebrand and also saved a woman's badly broken finger. With the bone exposed, most everyone would have expected an amputation. But

Charlie had cleaned the injury, set the bone and told the lady to come back in a few days so he could check for infection. With a little help from Bill's chloroform, the lady had dozed off during the most painful part of the procedure. Now everyone with an ailment, toothache or injury was eager to visit the Oriental Physician or dentist and see if they could get help for their own problem.

When Rachel got the door opened for the restaurant, she had several people file in ready to eat. She explained to them that the free meal was for Chinese food, which wasn't available until lunch time. Most promised to return, but a few went ahead and had breakfast, so she was soon busy with actual paying customers.

The fires were burning to heat the water at the laundry as their business also got off to a rousing start. It was like a traveling show had come to town and everyone wanted to see it.

Phoenix had a quick breakfast, watching with a measure of satisfaction, as Rachel and Su Lee handled the customers. Rachel was positively beaming as she served up ham and eggs, toast and coffee to table after table. Phoenix had her prepare an extra meal for his prisoner – mush and toast – and left while there were still six people at the tables.

Don Baylor was on the walk when he passed by. The mayor displayed a wide grin. 'Maybe I ought to put some advertising in the paper. Seems everyone in town has made their way down to your place this morning.'

'You get a paper?'

'Yes, and I've already told a lady, who helps us out on occasion, that we'll need her to watch the store come lunch time. Me and the wife are going to bring the kids over and try out your Chinese food.'

'Hope we don't run out of supplies before you get a shipment in.'

Don grew serious. 'Keep your eyes open,' he said quietly. 'That ruckus last night was no accident. My wife heard a rumor that the men from Hildebrand's ranch were told by Race Killroke to mix things up with the Slash T boys.'

Phoenix understood. 'Could have been a diversion, but Jody played it smart. He sent a runner for me and I had Bill go over to keep an eye on Blocker.'

'It still sounds like you best keep a sharp eye for trouble.'

The warning was not necessary, but Phoenix thanked him all the same. Jody had been watching for him at the jail and opened the door to greet him.

'Breakfast is being served at the Pomeroy House,' Phoenix informed him. 'You'll take your free meals there.' He walked past him and went to the cell where Blocker was waiting impatiently for breakfast. Seeing the mush and toast, he groaned.

'Sure do miss Martell and Nape. They brung me good food to eat.'

'If I see them, I'll remind them that they can still bring you a meal. There's no rule saying you have to eat what we provide for you.'

'Yeah?'

Phoenix gave him the bowl, a spoon and the plain chunk of bread. 'Besides, the judge will be here next week. Then you'll be going to a real hospitable place for your future meals – probably Canyon City.'

'The State Prison?' The color drained from his face. 'For hitting a guy once or twice?'

'Manslaughter is usually a jail sentence, and not thirty days doing odd jobs around town. I imagine you'll get a couple of years.'

Blocker appeared to have lost his appetite. 'Two years?'

'Hope Martell paid you extra for the beating you gave Grant Pomeroy.'

'Race said we had to. . . .' But Blocker realized his mouth was running by itself and closed his trap abruptly. Then he went to his bunk and sat down to eat.

'I'll watch the jail for a spell, Jody. You go get something to eat and rest up.'

'I got a little shut-eye last night, Phoenix. I'll be back to help out this afternoon.'

'That's fine, but the night duty is mine . . . unless there's trouble.'

'You're more than fair, Sheriff. I'll see you later.'

Even as Jody was leaving, Phoenix was thinking of

133

what Martell and Nape might be planning for their next attempt. With a circuit judge scheduled, they would need to break Blocker out of jail as soon as possible.

Charlie treated several stomach ailments, body aches and a couple minor injuries. Two women also complained of feminine discomfort, for which he prescribed his ginseng potion . . . with a caution to take but a small amount to control the worst of the pain.

It was well past noon when he stopped to get a bowl of chow mein at the restaurant. The place was packed and he ended up getting his own bowl from the kitchen and prepared to take it back to his office. Su Lee told him they had served nearly forty people and there were a few waiting for a place to sit. He took a moment to watch as Rachel took a copy of the newsletter from one man, plus the price of three more meals. He had his wife and two children with him. It was rewarding to see them all smiling when they spoke to Rachel about the 'funny looking' food that tasted so good. They promised to return, as the price – even without the free ad – was much less than any other place in town.

Fang Chow cut off his retreat from the room and pointed to Martell and Nape, standing outside the building. As yet, they had not interfered or tried to block anyone from coming to eat. It appeared they were just watching the place.

'Everything is going smooth so far,' he said to Charlie. 'But what do we do if someone starts trouble? I know our people are sometimes tormented by other races, because we are Chinese, and it has been customary to accept such abuse without fighting back.'

'This is not San Francisco, Fang Chow. Baihu is the law in Silver Springs. If trouble comes, send someone to fetch the deputy or Baihu.'

'And while we wait for help?'

'We are allowed to protect ourselves and this place,' Charlie said. 'If that means we must take up weapons and remove the troublemakers, that is what we must be prepared to do. A show of force is often sufficient, without actually going to battle.'

Fang Chow was incredulous. 'So much faith you put in Baihu.'

'And this land,' Charlie said. 'They have a creed which declares *all men are created equal.* This country endured a civil war so that all men could live free. Never has any other country in the history of the world done such a thing. We have men in this town who fought in that war. They supported the notion that every man has equal rights.'

'Maybe so, but they showed us only contempt in San Francisco.'

'Confucius once said: *Without feelings of respect, what is there to distinguish men from beasts?*' Charlie put on a stern expression. 'As men who have endured prejudice, we may have to earn that respect physically, but we shall have it.'

Fang Chow smiled his acceptance. 'I will tell the others to keep something near at hand, should we be forced to earn respect.'

'That's good, but if trouble comes, be sure to send for Baihu too.'

Race stormed inside the house, but suppressed his rancor when he saw Mrs Hildebrand was with Thurmond. He simmered just below a boil and forced himself to remain polite. The lady soon left the room and he was alone with his boss.

'You see the newsletter being handed out today?' Race cried. 'That crazy gunman is giving away free meals!'

'Very shrewd of him,' Hildebrand said. 'He brought out a copy to show me yesterday, before he sent his Chinese friend out to look at Mother.'

Race controlled his patience for another few, seemingly endless seconds. 'He do her any good?'

'She took a little medicine and slept soundly last night,' Hildebrand said, displaying satisfaction. 'And he suggested she eat more fruit and vegetables. The tonic he provided is supposed to help prevent the migraines, if she takes it at the first hint of a headache coming on. I imagine it has some of the same properties as laudanum, but it is better tasting and a swallow or two once in a while won't hurt her.'

Race took a deep breath and let it out slowly. 'So you've decided to let the whole bunch stay – the Chinese, Mrs Pomeroy, the dentist – all of them?'

'I'm sorry about the position I promised you, Race.' Hildebrand delivered the words with sincerity. 'I wanted the loading dock and pens too. But, unless something changes dramatically, I see no way for us to acquire the property we need.'

'How about picking a spot further down the track?'

'I'm going to sit back and enjoy what I have for a time. I need to think of my mother and I've already got enough to keep me busy.'

'What if something happens to Phoenix? I mean, I can't see a man like him settling down.'

'If he pulls out or moves with his Chinese, then we might have a chance of buying the Pomeroy House, perhaps by offering the lady a new boarding-house at the end of main street. However, I don't foresee such a thing happening. It's clear that Phoenix and the others have set up shop permanently.'

Race decided Hildebrand had made up his mind. He bit back rash or harsh words and kept his emotions hidden.

'All right then. I was just wondering if you'd seen the paper.'

'Yes, Mother and I are going into town for a late lunch. I believe I'll look over the new restaurant and laundry. Who knows? We might even like the food.'

'Whatever you say,' Race managed the words without allowing the bile he felt to surface. 'You're the boss.'

'Hitch the buggy for us, while I get Mother ready to go. She has only been to town once since she arrived. I think she'll enjoy the trip.'

Race swallowed his rancor and went to do what he was told. The plan to get Blocker out of jail had failed last night, but Martell swore he would get better results tonight. Whatever it took, he had to get rid of that two-bit gunman. The Chinese would move if threatened – same for the dentist. Then the boss could make nice with Mrs Pomeroy and build her a brand new boarding-house or something, that was up to him. But Race would have his own piece of the business, and rake in more money than he could ever spend. All that stood between him and his own little empire was Phoenix Cline!

CHAPTER EIGHT

Rachel had never dealt with so many people. Phoenix stopped by for a few minutes during the afternoon. He spoke to both Charlie and Bill, but Rachel was busy working and couldn't stop to chat. She did manage a quick wave and smile, happy he had come by to see how things were going. Then he was gone again and she had little time to concern herself about what he was up to.

As it neared closing time, and knowing Phoenix was going to be at the jail for the night, Rachel prepared his and Blocker's meals and placed them on a tray. She had been teaching Su how to take care of the money and the free meals during the day, so she felt the girl would be all right on her own for a few minutes.

Phoenix met her arrival at the jail with a smile. 'I almost forgot about supper,' he said. 'Blocker would have been real upset if you hadn't remembered to bring us something.'

'It ain't . . . uh, isn't much,' she said, correcting the wording. 'With Fang Chow using most of the stove for the Chinese food, I could only heat up a kettle of stew.'

'That will be fine.'

She entered the office and placed the tray on the desk. Once Phoenix had given a bowl of stew and large chunk of bread to Blocker, she sat down on one of the two chairs to wait.

'I could return these in the morning?' Phoenix offered.

Rachel shook her head. 'It's nice to relax for a few minutes. Besides, Su is tending the counter and knows how to make change.'

'Then you are getting a few paying customers?'

'More than I expected. Several families come by and even Mr Hildebrand and an elderly woman stopped in to eat.' She didn't mask her surprise. 'They tried most everything on the menu and then left us four-bits extra.'

Phoenix displayed a positive look. 'See? The man brought his mother to your restaurant. You have nothing more to fear from him.'

'Uh-huh,' she mocked his optimism. 'I'll believe that when dogs fly and chickens bay at the moon.'

Phoenix ate quickly, then retrieved the bowl from Blocker. The man didn't complain or offer a word. Rachel wondered about a bully like him being so subdued. When he glanced over at her, she thought she could detect a smirk, as if he knew something private and was pleased with the idea.

'Are you being real careful?' she asked Phoenix, once he had put his dish on the tray.

'You worried about me, ma'am?'

'I got reason to be worried,' she replied. 'If something happens to you, me and the Chinese will be at the mercy of Martell and Hildebrand again.'

He gave her a curious, yet bold sort of look. 'Are you sure that's the only reason?'

Rachel allowed a simper to play on her lips. 'You didn't actually say you wanted to court me, so maybe I don't have no more – I mean, *any* more – reasons.'

'I said I wasn't worthy to court someone as fine and decent as you, not that I didn't want to.'

She squirmed inwardly, but met his intense gaze unflinchingly. 'Well, I give you a hug, didn't I? Reckon that ought to tell you I don't give two hoots about your past.'

'Then I'd be honored if you'd allow me to court you proper, Mrs Pomeroy.'

Rachel gulped down her embarrassment from having forced the issue. She said a rapid: 'OK . . . bye!' And, with tray in hand, she whirled about and hurried out the door.

Darkness covered the town and Martell and Nape moved into position. A couple of boys he'd hired to

141

light some fireworks were due at any time. Martell had told them ten o'clock, so a good many people would be in bed. Things needed to appear quiet and normal until the explosions went off.

'Is them the kids?' Nape asked, pointing at several shadowy figures.

Martell squinted against the darkness and made out about a dozen phantoms, moving along the street in pairs or single-file. The parade marched along to the sheriff's office and entered through the door. As the men were exposed to light, Martell was able to identify them.

'It's the Chinese workers!' he exclaimed. 'What the devil is going on? It looks like every one of the coolies from the Pomeroy place is going to the jail.'

Phoenix met the men at the door and held it open, allowing all of them to crowd inside the office. He shut the door behind them and they remained inside for five minutes. Then the door opened and the Chinese came back out, moving the same as before, in pairs or single-file. It was baffling to watch and made no sense at all to Martell.

'Sneak over there and take a peek inside,' he told his ex-deputy, once the men were gone. 'Make sure all of those Chinese characters left.'

Nape kept to the darkness, until he could reach the walk. Then he eased along to the single window. It was shuttered, but there were cracks and a peephole for someone inside to keep watch outside

142

without being exposed to a bullet. After a short peruse, Nape tiptoed away and hurried back to where Martell was waiting.

'All clear, boss,' he said. 'Phoenix is at his desk and no one else is inside.'

'You sure Blocker knows we're coming tonight?'

'We whispered back and forth at the window when Jody was snoring last night. He don't want to go to prison. He'll do like you said.'

The window Nape spoke of, allowed light and air into the jail. The portals were seven feet off of the ground and each had three iron bars set in the mortar, but the opening was wide enough for passing through a gun.

The next hour passed slowly, without incident. Then the boys arrived with the fireworks. Moments later, they set off a dozen firecrackers and two rockets. It sounded like a major gunfight was going on in the middle of town.

Phoenix immediately doused the light inside the jail. Seconds later, he appeared at the door, partially hidden from view, with gun in hand, searching the darkness, trying to determine what was going on. With his attention on the street, Nape climbed on to a box in the alleyway and passed the gun through the back window to Blocker's cell. He leapt down, picked up the crate and hurried off into the darkness.

There was some shouting back and forth down near the fireworks display. Then someone called out that everything was fine, it was only some kids having fun.

Phoenix put away his gun and closed the door. A few seconds later, the lamp was relit.

Nape returned to stand at Martell's side, panting from completing his chore. 'Shouldn't be,' he puffed, winded from the exertion, 'long now.'

'Remember, we have to douse the lamp as soon as Blocker's cell door is unlocked. We don't want anyone seeing us. It's bad enough that Blocker has to leave the country. Once he's free, you and me will slip off to the Silver Palace and wait to hear the news. Won't be but a day or two and we will take back our old jobs.'

'Be sorry to lose Quade,' Nape said. 'He was handy in most any kind of fight.'

'Better to have his name on a wanted poster than for all three of us to be on the run.'

A shot suddenly cut the silent night, a blast from inside the jail!

'Let's go!' Martell shouted.

The two of them raced across the street and pushed through the door into the sheriff's office. Phoenix lay, unmoving, with his face and left arm on the desktop.

'The key!' Martell pointed to the nail where the cell key was kept.

Nape grabbed it and hurried back to open the cell. Martell went toward the lamp, to blow out the

144

light, when he heard Nape yelp in surprise.

Martell threw a look his direction. 'What the hell is. . . ?'

'Hold it!' Phoenix sat up erect, his gun pointed at Martell's chest.

Martell was dumb-struck. He gaped at Phoenix as Nape backed up with his hands raised. Both of them dropped their guns.

Bill Williams came out of Blocker's cell. He had a gun trained on the two ex-lawmen and a smile on his face. 'Worked like a charm,' he said to Phoenix.

'What'd you do to Blocker?' Martell wanted to know. 'Why didn't he warn us?'

'Bill put him to sleep about an hour ago,' Phoenix informed him. 'He used chloroform.'

'How the devil did you get here?' Nape asked the dentist.

'I dressed up as one of the Chinese,' Bill revealed the subterfuge. 'You should have counted bodies. Eleven Chinese entered, but only ten went out again.'

'Remove your gun belts,' Phoenix ordered. 'Bill, check them for any other weapons and put them in the cell next to Blocker.'

A few minutes later, Phoenix thanked Bill and the dentist left the office. Martell was still growling over their plan going awry.

'Quit your whining, Martell, or you'll get nothing but bread and water until the judge gets here.'

145

'You've got nothing on us,' Martell retorted. 'We heard the shot and run in to see if you were all right.'

'Yes, and you were so concerned about my welfare, you immediately had Nape grab the key to let Blocker out of his cell,' Phoenix rebuked him. 'You stick to your story, Martell. The judge might have himself a good laugh.'

'Your days are numbered, Cline,' Martell snarled the words. 'You walk tall while you can, but your time is coming.'

'Did Hildebrand put you up to this?'

'I ain't saying nothing,' Martell sneered.

'Might go easier on you if you confessed,' Phoenix advised him.

But Nape and Martell kept their silence.

Phoenix barred the door and turned the lamp down for the night. There was a cot on one side of the office, so he could doze off and still be available for any problems that might arise. He was glad his plan had worked. No one was hurt and two more troublemakers were behind bars.

Race had slipped away without Hildebrand or anyone else being the wiser. The news of the attempted jailbreak was all over town. Martell and Nape were cellmates, along with Blocker, and all three would be on trial within a week. The clumsy buffoons were about as useful as three blind mice. Worse, one of them might panic and point their finger at him. He had to act quickly, before that happened.

He took up watching Phoenix from nearby buildings and stayed out of sight. The notion paid off that afternoon. The sheriff and the Pomeroy woman went for a walk, with him carrying a basket, down toward the nearby creek. It appeared they intended to have themselves a private picnic.

Race let them get nearly out of sight before he made his way along the same path. Once Phoenix was sitting down on a blanket, engrossed by the moderately attractive Mrs Pomeroy, he would have his chance. Martell and his clown friends had made a mess of things. This time he would take matters in his own hands.

Race heard the soft sounds of their voices before he spied the pair. They had picked a grassy spot under a mature cottonwood tree, sitting side by side, while eating their meal. From the scent on the breeze, it smelled like fried chicken.

Race sought a better vantage point, but the area was open, with only a few stands of bunch grass and a small thicket of wild rose nearby. The solitary tree beneath which they were sitting, was the only good place for cover within a hundred yards. He was still fifty or sixty steps away, much too far for his handgun.

Should have brought your rifle, stupid! he cussed his lack of forethought.

However, Phoenix had his back to him, and Mrs Pomeroy seemed to have eyes only for the man at her side. They had chosen to sit facing the stream, which was thirty feet down a gentle slope – probably thinking it was more romantic. For whatever reason, it allowed him to make a careful approach, using what cover there was and easing forward a few steps at a time.

His chance came when the pair paused from eating. They leaned toward one another and shared a diffident kiss. Race made his decision and rushed forward, his gun ready for use!

Phoenix instantly became aware of him and hastily pushed Rachel out of the way. His protective reaction gave Race a clean shot – he took it!

Phoenix was knocked over from the bullet's impact. The lady screamed in shock, and Race fired again and again, desperate to finish him off. But Phoenix rolled down the slight hill and he knew he'd missed.

Race continued his charge, seeking to get off a final kill-shot. He saw that blood covered the right side of the man's shirt, but Phoenix still managed to get his gun free. He was at an awkward position, trying to steady the gun with his left hand. . . .

Race skidded to a stop and took aim; he had only one or two bullets left. He had to make certain of his next round. But it was the wrong strategy by a split-second. As he squeezed the trigger, a white hot lead missile tore through his chest. His shot was ruined and, before he could fire again, he was struck twice more.

Something was terribly wrong. Race stared through a red haze and could see nothing but grass! He realized he was lying face down a few feet from a picnic blanket. He had no feeling above the waist, although his legs kept pumping, as if he was running. Suddenly, the wind and energy left his body. A deep sigh escaped through his mouth and he deflated like a punctured balloon. His last moment of consciousness allowed a final thought: *Ye gods, Race! Mrs Hildebrand probably shoots straighter than you!*

Phoenix didn't pass out until Charlie was standing over him with a knife. Then a damp, cloyingly sweet cloth was placed over his nose and mouth. As he lost consciousness, bits of wild dreams floated through his head. Afterwards, came the utter tranquility of sleep.

Pain is a great indicator that a man is still alive. Phoenix came awake to discover the room in total darkness and his right side felt on fire. He must have moaned in his effort to regain awareness, as a lamp's glow abruptly bathed the room in light.

'You about scared me to death,' Rachel's voice came from the side of the bed. 'Charlie kept saying you'd be all right, but I seen all the blood and I.. . . .' Her voice cracked with emotion.

'You gave me the best kiss of my life,' he said, able to see her leaning over his bed. 'I won't be going anywhere until I try that again.'

'You . . . you've got no more brains than a daisy!' she snapped. 'Race almost killed you, and you're still romancing me!'

'I've got to try and win your hand any time I have the chance,' he clarified. 'With Bill and maybe a bunch more suitors chasing after you, I can't let up for a second.'

Rachel's expression softened. 'I done spoke to Bill, whilst I was waiting for you to come around. He asked if I was serious about you and I told him yes.'

'You did?'

'I let you kiss me!' she said hotly. 'I never let no one kiss me before. Even Grant never kissed me like he cared anything for me.'

'You'll pardon me saying so, but Grant was a fool.'

'Well, anyway, Bill said he had no hard feelings against you. He had already figured out that I was fond of you or tetched . . . or both.'

Phoenix attempted to move his right arm, but the pain was too great. He grit his teeth against the searing wave of agony that washed over him for the second time. 'How bad is it?' he asked, breathless from the effort required not to cry out.

'Charlie says you won't be able to use your right arm for some time. He thinks some of the damage might be permanent.'

'Well, I was looking to hang up my gun.'

The whisper of a smile played on Rachel's lips as she leaned closser to look down at him. 'What will you do to earn a living?'

He grinned, enjoying her nearness. 'Thought I might find myself a rich widow and settle down.'

'I ain't ... uh, am not rich.' A pixie-like smile danced on her lips. 'But I do own half an interest in a boarding-house and restaurant.'

'You two can discuss your future when Baihu is adequately rested,' Charlie's stern, father-like voice filled the room.

Phoenix turned his head enough to see the man had come to stand at the foot of the bed. 'Charlie,' he complained, 'I can't say much for your timing. I was about to get myself a goodnight kiss.'

Charlie did an about-turn and put his back to them. 'Proceed quickly please, Mrs Pomeroy. I will check for bleeding and Baihu must get his sleep.'

Rachel hesitated, but Phoenix wasn't going to let her escape. 'Come on, little darlin', kiss me good-night,' he coaxed. 'Daddy's got to tuck me in.'

She blushed brightly, but lowered her head and gave him a quick peck on the lips. Then she hurried out of the room.

Charlie came to his side, removed the blankets and examined his wound. 'Good, no blood has soaked through. I believe you will survive to be as big a nuisance tomorrow as you were yesterday.'

'My right arm feels heavy,' Phoenix told Charlie. 'It's like the muscles don't work quite right.'

'The bullet went through at an angle, upwards through your arm and lodged in your shoulder. I extracted the bullet, but I believe you may have some lingering – even permanent – restrictions on the use of the arm.'

'It could have been a lot worse,' Phoenix admitted. 'I rolled when I got hit and Race missed me three or four times. If we hadn't been sitting at the top of the rise, he would have had me cold.'

'Well, you managed to get the best of him. He was dead when I arrived.'

'I was durn lucky. Any more trouble since I've been unconscious?'

'No. Mr Hildebrand stopped by. He said Race acted on his own. He had promised Race a lucrative position if the loading docks were built. He thinks the man must have thought getting rid of you would turn things around.'

'I'm glad Race didn't hit Rachel by mistake. Shooting wild like he was, she was in more danger than me.'

'Get some sleep, Baihu.'

'Might have to change the name you call me, Charlie. I'll not be much of a white tiger without the use of my gun hand. What's the name for *helpless white kitten?*'

Charlie grinned. 'Good night . . . Baihu.'

CHAPTER NINE

The four men entered town and soon learned the condition of Phoenix Cline. He had been shot less than a week ago and his right arm was in a sling. Within minutes, Zeke Lichen and his men took Phil and Irene Douglas hostage. It was Don Baylor who arrived at the boarding-house to speak to Phoenix.

'It's Zeke and some of his boys?' Phoenix confirmed.

'Got three men with him – Chips, Ivan and Stummer, were the names Zeke mentioned. He says they will meet you on the main street of town in fifteen minutes. If you don't show, they'll kill Mr Douglas. Ten minutes after that, they'll kill Mrs Douglas.'

Charlie had been privy to the conversation. He had a very worried look on his face. 'The odds are very long without the use of your right arm.'

Phoenix was already strapping on a pair of guns

. . . though it was awkward working with only one hand. 'I used to wear two guns, back when I started my life as Phoenix Cline,' he said. 'I still had the dual holsters put away.'

'But there are four of them,' Don objected. 'You can't go up against four men all by yourself.'

'It's my fight, Mayor. I killed Zeke's brother. I'm the one he came after.'

Don was about to speak again, but Charlie held up a hand to stop him. 'It is the way of Baihu, Mayor. You must let him do this. It is his destiny.'

'Destiny?' Don cried. 'He'll get himself killed!'

But Charlie escorted the mayor out of the room. He then had to stop Rachel from entering. She had also heard the news.

'Trust me this one time,' he spoke firmly to her. 'Baihu must finish the fight he started in San Francisco. You cannot interfere.'

'But, Charlie,' she said, her eyes filling with tears. 'I can't watch him get killed. He's the first man I ever. . . .' she groped for the right words, 'that I ever really loved.'

'I care for him like a son myself,' Charlie replied. 'I'm telling you now, you must let him have this last battle, so that he might never have to fight again.'

Rather than make a worse scene, Rachel turned and ran up to her room.

Phoenix felt the sharp stab of regret. He had sorely wanted to hold Rachel one last time. 'You

154

don't really think I can take Zeke and three men, do you, Charlie?'

'Confucius says: *Virtue is not left to stand alone. He who practices it will have neighbors.*'

'Sometimes you can be awfully vague.'

Charlie mustered up a tight smile. 'Trust me, my son. It is time you put the life of Phoenix Cline to rest. This is how it must be.'

Phoenix checked the loads in his gun and slipped it back into the holster. He was at a disadvantage, but he wasn't going to let innocent people die. He took a deep breath and let it out slowly.

'Guess it's about time,' he said. Then he started the long walk to Main Street.

Zeke was waiting on the porch of the news office. Chips was close at his side, while Strummer and Ivan were standing inside the open door. Phil and Irene were sitting on chairs next to Irene's desk.

'Yonder he comes,' Chips spoke up. 'Looks like his right arm is still in a sling.'

'Word around town is he won't ever draw with that hand again,' Strummer drawled. 'This ought to be like shooting ducks on a pond.'

'Let's not be standoffish, boys,' Zeke jeered. 'Let's step out and meet the famous gunman proper like . . . before we blow him to hell!'

The four men spread out on the street as they faced the legendary Phoenix Cline. With several feet between each of them, it would make it doubly tough on a single opponent, even if he did manage to get off a shot or two.

Phoenix walked forward until he was forty feet away. He stopped and there was a dead silence for a few seconds.

'You killed my brother, Cline,' Zeke boomed the words. 'I'm here to see you lying in a pool of your own blood.'

'Missed your chance there,' Phoenix replied. 'You should have been here a couple days ago.'

'Well, this is going to be more permanent. You won't be walking away from. . . .'

Phoenix wondered why the man had stopped in mid-sentence. He risked a sidelong glance and saw the reason . . . in fact twelve of them!

Charlie and all eleven of the Chinese men were carrying clubs. They hurried on to the main street and closed to within a few steps of the four gunmen. Six of them flanked Zeke and his men on either side, poised, ready to attack.

'If you want revenge for your brother, you have your chance,' Charlie told Zeke. 'But if any of your friends interfere, we will strike all of you down without mercy.'

Zeke stared in awe at the Chinese men. Indeed, they had murderous looks on their faces and held their clubs ready for use.

'I'm here to see it's a fair fight too,' Jody had

slipped along the walk and was in front of the general store. At his side was Don Baylor, who had a shotgun in his hands.

'That goes for me too,' Don said. 'You already have an unfair advantage with Phoenix being wounded.'

Before Phoenix had time to think or argue with the pair, Bill Williams arrived with Thurmond Hildebrand and four of his men on horseback. They also had guns.

Hildebrand put his hand on his butt of his pistol and spoke up. 'You men aren't such cowards that it takes four of you to take on a one-armed, injured man?'

'This isn't you people's fight, it doesn't concern any of you,' Phoenix said. 'I don't want anyone else to get hurt.'

'We got a telegram yesterday,' Jody was the one to answer back. 'These four are wanted for robbery in California. It seems that, after you killed Zack and eliminated his band of bullies, people started to feel safer about telling the law about his brother here. The Lichen boys walked roughshod over everyone while they were ramroding two different gangs, but that's over now.'

Phoenix smiled, realizing the meaning of the last Confucius quote Charlie had made – *a man who practices virtues has neighbors.* He concentrated on Zeke, no longer concerned about the other three men.

'What'll it be, Lichen?' Phoenix made the offer. 'I'm placing all four of you under arrest, but I'll give you a chance at me.'

Zeke sneered back at him. 'Just you? You're gonna draw on me, wounded like you are?'

Phoenix replied, 'I never favored using my left hand, but I'm not going to look over my shoulder for you the rest of my life.'

Zeke took a moment to check with his men. They had already decided these were not the kind of odds they had anticipated. As one, the three of them lifted their hands. A lane was open between Zeke and Phoenix, and Chips gave his pal a nod.

'You can take him, Zeke. He's stove up and can't use his regular gun hand.'

'That's right,' Strummer added. 'He ain't got a prayer against you left-handed.'

Zeke snorted his contempt. 'Prepare to visit my brother . . . in hell!' With his last words, he clawed for his gun—

Phoenix fired twice as the man's pistol cleared its holster. Both bullets scored hits to his chest, driving him back a step with each round. Zeke couldn't keep his feet under him and sat down, losing his gun when he hit the ground. Then, for a long moment, he stared blindly, a look of utter incredulity on his face.

'Y-you said . . . you didn't . . . favor. . . . .' But his life's force waned and he lost the power of speech.

'I said I didn't favor using my left hand, Zeke,'

Phoenix told him, holstering his gun. 'I didn't say I didn't know how to shoot with that hand.'

It was questionable whether the words reached Zeke before he died. He fell over on his side and the three other gang members were taken into custody by Jody and Bill.

'Going to be crowded until that judge arrives,' Jody remarked to Phoenix. 'Good thing we'll be sending these three to San Francisco to stand trial.'

'I'll be over to relieve you tonight,' Phoenix told him.

'Not tonight you won't!' a woman's voice barked. 'You are going back to bed until you are fully recovered.'

Charlie and the rest of the Chinese headed back to the Pomeroy House to resume their duties. Hildebrand lifted a hand in farewell and led his men out of town. Two men carted off Zeke's body to the undertaker, and Phoenix was left alone on the street with Rachel.

'I swear, you're going to need watching all the time,' she declared. 'Soon as you marry me, we're going to get some rules straight about you carrying a badge and risking getting yourself killed.'

Phoenix grinned. 'Didn't the mayor tell you? There's going to be an election for sheriff next month. I don't intend to be on the ballot.'

Rachel marched up to him and stopped mere inches away. 'And that's supposed to make every-

159

thing OK? You come out here to get yourself shot to pieces and leave me worrying if you'll even survive. I'm not gonna' put up with that any more. I mean it!'

Phoenix reached out, using his good left arm, and pulled her to him. 'You sometimes talk too much, lady,' he said. Then he kissed her soundly on the lips.

After several blissful seconds, Rachel pulled back from him. She had a dreamy look in her eyes. 'Ain't you got no shame?' she asked impishly. 'Everyone will think we are already engaged.'

Phoenix didn't correct her using the word ain't. 'Let them think what they want,' he said, leaning back to look down at her lovely face. 'Soon as I can buy me a suit, I'll drag you in front of a preacher.'

Rachel laughed. 'You ain't. . . .' she paused to correct her speech this time, 'aren't as smart as Charlie says you are . . . not if you think you'll have to drag me anywhere. But once we're married proper, your gun-toting days are over.'

'Yeah,' Phoenix agreed. 'I can live with that.'